CHERRY AMES,

JUNGLE NURSE

WHEN Cherry Ames is offered a temporary assignment to help establish a health clinic in a small native African village, she sees it as a once-in-a-lifetime opportunity. Not only will she be visiting a strange and exciting part of the world—but, more importantly, she will have a chance to help the underprivileged people of a semiprimitive country.

But no sooner has the clinic been built than Cherry finds herself caught up in the midst of a mysterious chain of events. Rough diamonds are being smuggled out of Africa—and Cherry's acute observations lead her to believe that the clinic itself is the base of the smugglers' operations!

By carefully putting together obscure bits and pieces of evidence, and at great personal danger to herself, Cherry sets a trap for the criminals.

How the alert young nurse from the United States manages to put an end to an international smuggling ring provides a whirlwind finish to a fascinating story of mystery and intrigue.

The CHERRY AMES *Nurse Stories*

Student Nurse
Senior Nurse
Army Nurse
Chief Nurse
Flight Nurse
Veterans' Nurse
Private Duty Nurse
Visiting Nurse
Cruise Nurse
At Spencer
Night Supervisor
Mountaineer Nurse

Clinic Nurse
Dude Ranch Nurse
Rest Home Nurse
Country Doctor's Nurse
Boarding School Nurse
Department Store Nurse
Camp Nurse
At Hilton Hospital
Island Nurse
Rural Nurse
Staff Nurse
Companion Nurse

Jungle Nurse

The VICKI BARR *Flight Stewardess Series*

Silver Wings for Vicki
Vicki Finds the Answer
The Hidden Valley Mystery
The Secret of Magnolia
   Manor
The Clue of the Broken
   Blossom
Behind the White Veil
The Mystery at Hartwood
   House
Peril Over the Airport

The Mystery of the
   Vanishing Lady
The Search for the
   Missing Twin
The Ghost at the
   Waterfall
The Clue of the
   Gold Coin
The Silver Ring Mystery
The Clue of the
   Carved Ruby

The Mystery of Flight 908
The Brass Idol Mystery

From inside the tent came the murmur of voices

CHERRY AMES
JUNGLE NURSE

By

HELEN WELLS

~~~~~~

NEW YORK

GROSSET & DUNLAP

Publishers

Contents

CHAPTER   PAGE

I THE TOWER OF LONDON 1

II JET TO AFRICA 12

III NAIROBI 31

IV NGOGO 47

V DIAMONDS AGAIN 66

VI KANDI 76

VII THE ORANGE AIRPLANE 92

VIII THE PRETTY PEBBLE 99

IX VISITORS 109

X THE YELLOW STONE 121

XI THE TEST TUBES 139

XII ADDING IT UP 151

XIII THE WHITE HUNTER 158

XIV THE END OF THE STORY 173

CHAPTER I

~~~~~~

The Tower of London

IT WAS A FOGGY DAY IN THE ANCIENT CITY OF LON-
don. Curling wisps of mist, blown in from the
Thames, washed up against the windows of the
double-decker bus as it lumbered along the twists and
turns of celebrated Baker Street.

Sitting hunched over in the front seat of the top
deck, Cherry Ames peered through the haze at the old
stone buildings that lined the street, and wondered if
one of them might be the famous 221-B where Sherlock Holmes and Dr. Watson had their rooms. Because of the fog, it was impossible for Cherry to see the
number plates over the doors. It was from 221-B that
the great detective set out at all hours of the day and
night to solve the robberies and murder mysteries that
always seemed to baffle the police.

Cherry had been involved in so many mysteries
herself that Holmes, with his long, plaid cape and

1

deerstalker cap, seemed almost real to her. For a fleeting moment she wondered if she might run into another mystery when she got back home. But she quickly dismissed the thought. Hilton, Illinois was such a quiet, typical Midwest town that it hardly seemed likely.

It was Cherry's last day in England. For the past month, as companion nurse to the American writer, Martha Logan, Cherry had traveled all through the English countryside. But now her temporary assignment was finished—as was the research that Mrs. Logan had been doing for a book—and at last it was time for both of them to return to the States, and for Cherry to get back to her job at Hilton Hospital. Even in a prosperous American town like Hilton, there never seemed to be enough nurses.

So, on this final afternoon in London, she was having one last fling at sightseeing.

The bus turned from Baker Street into Oxford Street, which was crowded with big department stores and small shops, and, in spite of the weather, jammed with people. Londoners were so used to fog, Cherry thought, that it took a real pea-souper to keep them indoors. Taxis, cars, trucks, and buses were crawling along bumper to bumper.

Then, as they emerged into Trafalgar Square, the fog began to lift, and Cherry could plainly see the statue of Lord Nelson standing on top of its towering pedestal. Up Ludgate Hill the bus went, past the magnificent dome of St. Paul's Cathedral, and through a maze of narrow streets to the jumble of weathered gray-stone buildings that is known as the Tower of London.

Cherry had read all about the Tower in a guide-book and was determined to see it in a leisurely way. She knew that it was a living symbol of English history. William the Conqueror had built the original tower, and later kings had added other towers and moats and walls. In these grim dungeons, Anne Boleyn and the Earl of Essex had lost their heads to the executioner's ax; and Sir Walter Raleigh and a long list of other famous people whose names fill the history books had spent dreary years in prison. Now the Tower was a national museum which contained many of England's most precious relics, including the priceless Crown Jewels.

Cherry alighted from the bus, gaped for a moment at the Grenadier Guard, who, in a bright-red coat and tall bearskin hat, was marching stiffly up and down before the main entrance, and then she went in through the arched stone gateway.

For the next hour, she lost herself completely in the fabulous exhibits, wandering from room to room amid a crowd of other tourists. Most of them she recognized as fellow Americans, not only by their accents as they spoke to each other but also by the cameras hung around their necks.

In one room she saw what was probably the most

curious exhibit of all. Two mannikin knights were seated side by side on mannikin horses, both dressed in suits of shining steel armor. One of the knights was trim and slim; and the other was hugely fat. Cherry couldn't suppress a giggle when a guide explained to the crowd that both suits had been made for King Henry the Eighth—the first when he was a boy of nineteen, the second when he was a middle-aged man and had indulged himself too freely at too many banquet tables.

Behind her a man's voice, distinctly American, seemed to echo her thoughts. "The old boy should have watched his calorie intake," the voice said. "He should have had a good nurse looking after him. Somebody like Cherry Ames."

Cherry wheeled around, her eyes as wide as saucers, then she laughed.

"Well, for goodness' sake!" she gasped. "If it isn't Bob Barton, the millionaire intern!"

Bob grinned. "In the flesh," he assured her. "But what in the world are you doing here in London? I didn't think nurses ever had time for European vacations."

"It's a long story," Cherry said. "And I was going to ask you the same thing. The last I heard, you had finished your internship and were doing resident work."

"Well, mine's a long story too. But if you've had enough sightseeing, I'll take you some place and buy you tea and a crumpet and we can tell our long stories to each other."

"That," Cherry declared, "is the best offer I've had today. Besides, my feet are killing me from tramping over these hard stone floors."

"Then face about and quick march," Bob said, affecting an English accent, "and Ho for the Blue Bird Inn!"

Cherry had met Bob Barton a year or so before, when she had been on a special private-duty assignment at St. Luke's Hospital in New York, and he had been serving the last few months of his internship. His father, she had learned, was one of the richest oil-well operators in Texas. But Bob had passed up the idle life of a millionaire playboy for a more satisfying one in medicine. The other interns at St. Luke's had jokingly referred to him as the "millionaire intern," and Bob had gone along good-naturedly with the gag. But Cherry had soon learned that beneath his lighthearted, wisecracking exterior, Bob Barton was one of the most dedicated young doctors she had ever known.

The Blue Bird was an old-fashioned inn in Eastcheap, only a short walk from the Tower. Its oak paneling glowed with the patina of age, and Cherry guessed that the oaken chairs and tables were nearly as old as the inn itself.

"All of a sudden I'm hungry," Cherry said. She pointed across the room to where a chef in a tall white cap was carving a loin of beef. "May I have a cold beef sandwich instead of just a crumpet?"

"You name it and it's yours," Bob said. "They didn't kid me about being a millionaire for nothing." He ordered for both of them.

When the sandwiches and steaming mugs of tea arrived, Bob said, "All right, give. What is Cherry Ames doing in London?"

As she ate her sandwich and drank her tea, Cherry explained all about the assignment that had brought her to England.

"But now it's over," she added. "Tomorrow morning, bright and early, Mrs. Logan and I are flying back to New York."

As she talked, Bob's face had grown serious. "Look here, Cherry," he said. "You asked me for my story, and I am now going to tell it at some length. And when I'm finished I'm going to ask you to do one of the most important things you have ever done in your life."

Cherry's brow wrinkled in curiosity. But she kept silent as Bob went on talking.

"It's like this," Bob began. "When I finished my internship at St. Luke's, the hospital offered me a residency. And I was about to take it when I ran into a fellow I had gone to med school with. He was with the Abercrombie Foundation, and he gave me a tremendous pitch about all the good work they are doing all over the world among underprivileged people."

"The Abercrombie Foundation? That's a privately endowed organization, isn't it?"

"Yes," Bob said. "Old Mr. Abercrombie made his millions in chemicals. And when he died, about ten years ago, he left the bulk of his estate for the establishment of a medical foundation to help people who can't help themselves. You know, just as Carnegie left his money to establish libraries."

Cherry nodded. She knew about the Abercrombie Foundation, of course, but had never had occasion to come into actual contact with it.

"Anyhow," Bob went on, "I liked the idea of working with an outfit like that, so the upshot was that I applied for the next vacancy on their staff. And after an interview or two, I was accepted, and assigned to their Washington hospital. That was just a year ago."

Bob took a sip of his tea.

"I said this was a long story, but I'm going to try to cut it as short as I can. You may not remember, but I was always sort of a nut on tropical diseases, and at the Foundation Hospital we saw plenty—mostly civilian workers coming back from duty in Asia and Africa. I began to study up on them, and finally decided to make it my specialty.

"Now comes the reason I'm here in London. About a month ago we got an SOS from the Foundation representative in Kenya, East Africa. It appears that a fairly serious epidemic of trypanosomiasis has broken out among the Kikuyu natives in a little village"—he stopped a moment to remember—"called Ngogo, if I'm pronouncing it correctly. It's down near the Tanganyika border."

Cherry recognized the medical term. "Sleeping sickness! But I thought that had been pretty well wiped out in Africa!"

"Well," Bob said thoughtfully, "it had. As you know, it's caused by the bite of the tsetse fly, and in the old days it was a dread killer of cattle and humans alike. Then the British Health Service moved in and got it under control by destroying the breeding places of the tsetse. But a few years ago Kenya became an independent nation, and the British hygienic teams gradually began pulling out of the country."

Cherry frowned. "And left those poor people without any help at all?"

"It's not quite as simple as that," Bob explained. "About nine-tenths of the whole African continent has become independent in recent years. And the Africans are a very proud people. Kenya had quite a few English-trained native doctors, but not nearly enough to take care of five or six million people— mostly pretty primitive by our standards—and scattered over nearly a quarter of a million square miles of bush and hill country. When this epidemic struck, it was a much bigger thing than the native Kenyan medical organization could handle, so the government in Nairobi asked us for help."

The waiter came by with a fresh pot of tea. After he had freshened their cups, Bob went on.

"As you know," he said, "the Abercrombie Foundation operates wherever help is needed, especially in the newly developing countries. So since I happened to be something of a specialist in tropical diseases, I got tabbed for this African assignment."

Cherry's eyes lighted up. "Africa! What an opportunity for a doctor—a nurse! Think of what you could do for people, and learn! I almost wish I was going with you."

"That's what I was coming to," Bob said seriously. "I brought a nurse with me from the States. But last evening, only a few hours after we had arrived, she got a cable to the effect that her mother back in Virginia had suffered a stroke. That meant she had to take the next flight home, which sort of left me in the lurch. I burned up the wires to Washington this morning; but assigning a replacement for her, going through all that organizational red tape, and getting her over here takes more time than I can afford. So I went sightseeing this afternoon to take my mind off my troubles. Then when I saw you in the Tower, it seemed as though the answer had been sent to me like a gift from Heaven."

Cherry's dark eyes widened. "Me?"

"Yes—you, Cherry. I want you to replace my nurse and come to Kenya with me. When I was at St. Luke's, I had a chance to see how you worked, and

I'd much rather have you than some nurse out of the replacement pool that I've never even met. Besides, it will save a lot of time." He grinned. "Well, what do you say?"

Cherry's mouth hung open. "Why—why, Bob," she said, hesitating, "you really sweep a girl off her feet." Then she thought awhile and shook her head. "No—no, I don't see how I can. I'm due back at Hilton, and they really need me there. The supervisor of nurses is expecting me the end of this week."

"See here, my girl," Bob said earnestly. "They don't need you half as much back in Illinois as those poor Kikuyus out in Kenya do. I can fix it up in two shakes of the Atlantic cable. I'll wire your supervisor and tell her about the emergency. Then I'll buzz Washington for official approval. And I'll bet you King Henry's two suits of armor that both O.K.'s come through in no time."

Cherry's pretty head was spinning. The idea of going to such a strange, faraway place as Africa was making her heart beat fast.

"I don't know, Bob," she said slowly. "You could wait for your substitute nurse from Washington, and . . ."

But by the hesitant tone of her voice, young Dr. Robert Barton knew that he had won.

"No, I can't, Cherry," he assured her. "You know how I work, and I know how you work." Bob took her hand in his. "We'd make a terrific team, Cherry. And if you think it was a challenge working with junior volunteers back in America, just think how much more satisfaction you'll get training native nurses out in Kenya."

"Take me back to my hotel," Cherry said, "and I'll think it over."

"That's a deal," Bob said, grinning. "We'll grab a taxi and you can be thinking it over on the way. By the time we reach the hotel, you will have made up your mind to come to Africa. Then I'll get those cables going." His voice grew more serious. "The thing is, Cherry, we don't have any time to waste. This Kenya business is urgent."

Cherry smiled, and her eyes twinkled.

"All right, Bob," she said. "You're the doctor."

~~~~~~

CHAPTER II

Jet to Africa

TWO AFTERNOONS LATER, CHERRY AND BOB BARTON sat in the big waiting room at London Airport, looking out through the large observation window. They watched the flowing tendrils of fog that had settled down once more over the city.

Yesterday and this morning had been hectic. First, Cherry had seen Mrs. Logan off on her return flight to the States, pleased that the writer had now recovered sufficiently to be able to travel alone. Then she had gone to the American consulate and had her passport visaed for Africa. And her arm still ached a little from the shots she had taken as a precaution against tropical diseases.

Back at her hotel, she at once cabled her family about her sudden change of plans, and followed it with a long airmail letter spelling out all the details. Next, she wrote an even longer letter to the other nurses back at the Spencer Club in New York. She was sure that Josie, Mai Lee, Bertha, and all the other girls would be absolutely green with envy at the idea of her exploring such a faraway place as Africa. She knew that when they had read the letter they would be buzzing about it among themselves for weeks. She must remember, she decided, to send them regular reports.

While Cherry was busy with her own correspondence, Bob had gotten off his cables to the States. He had wired the supervisor of nurses at Hilton Hospital, who promptly extended Cherry's leave of absence "in a good cause," as she put it. Then he received a cable from the Abercrombie Foundation in Washington giving Bob carte blanche in choosing an assistant for his Kenya assignment.

Cherry wondered about what additional clothes or uniforms she should buy.

"Forget it," Bob advised her. "We're going back into some pretty rough country, so we'll be wearing bush clothes practically all the time. I'm afraid there'll be no place in Ngogo for pretty, white nurses' uniforms. There are Arab tailors in Nairobi who can fix us up in a jiffy. Each one of them has a staff of about twenty people who measure their customers in the morning, and have all the outfits they want ready for them that same afternoon." He smiled. "And the amazing thing is that they fit almost as well as if you'd had them made on Fifth Avenue in New York."

The African trip, Cherry thought to herself, was sounding more exciting every moment.

But now, as Cherry gazed out over the fogged-in airstrip, she sighed. "Do you suppose we're going to be held up all day?"

"Oh, no," Bob told her. "Some of the flights for the States may be grounded pending weather reports over the Atlantic. But the skies are pretty sure to be bright and blue over the Channel and northern France. So we ought to take off on schedule."

All over the big room, people were milling around, asking endless questions at the information desks, and checking their watches impatiently with the big clock on the wall. Ranged around the big clock were smaller clocks that told the time at that moment in New York, San Francisco, Berlin, Cairo, Bombay, and half a dozen other important cities throughout the world.

Cherry found herself glancing at her own watch too. Now that she had got used to the idea of going to Africa, she couldn't wait to be on her way.

Suddenly the loudspeaker overhead began to squawk.

"Attention, please! Attention, please!" The voice sounded like that of a mechanical man. "East African Airways Flight 14, bound for Cairo, Nairobi, Johannesburg, and Capetown, now loading at Portal Five. Repeat. East African Airways . . ."

Cherry jumped up. "Come on," she said, her eyes sparkling. "That's us. Let's go."

Bob took her arm and the two made their way out of the waiting room through the bustling crowd to the loading ramp.

"Let's get on early," Bob suggested, "and grab a seat up forward, where we can get a view—if there is any view to get. These jets fly too high to see much of anything, but at least you may be able to catch a glimpse of the Alps if there isn't too much low cloud cover."

The big jet sat silently on the runway, shrouded in gray fog, as the two found their way to a pair of forward seats and settled into them. The tip of the long wing behind them disappeared into the mist, and all Cherry could see of the terminal building were rows of dim lights, blurred by the haze.

"Br-r!" Cherry said, with a mock shiver. "It's a little spooky taking off like this when you can't see where you're going."

"Don't worry," Bob said. "Taking off in a fog is no problem. It's landing that can be a real problem. The fact that we're ready to go on time means that the weather is clear over the Channel."

Cherry looked around at the passengers entering the plane. There was a scattering of people who were unmistakably Americans. Then two Indians, in army uniforms, with white turbans on their heads and heavy black beards, took seats directly behind them. A number of dark-skinned Africans, wearing European clothes and carrying briefcases, filed up the aisle. One

African, who looked as if he might be an official of one of the new governments, wore a brightly colored robe and carried an ornate fly whisk under his arm, in much the same manner as a London businessman carries his umbrella.

Then Cherry heard the plane's doors being closed, and almost at once the jet engines, one by one, began their curious whine. Slowly the plane began to move forward through the fog. In an instant the dim lights of the terminal building were gone, and up ahead Cherry could see the rows of runway markers, turned by the murk from bright red to pale pink. Then the shrill engine whine grew louder as the jet gathered speed, and Cherry could feel it lift off the ground. Instantly the whine of the engines was gone, and the ship slid silently through the foggy air.

For about ten minutes the big jetliner continued to climb. Then suddenly it shot out of the fog and into dazzling sunlight. Below her, Cherry could see the neat fields of England, ending abruptly in high white cliffs, and beyond them the sparkling waters of the English Channel.

"See," Bob said, "I told you we'd have good flying weather."

As the jet climbed higher, the outlines of the waves below grew more indistinct. They flew over the coast of France, and the villages beneath them showed up as not much more than brown spots on the green landscape. A few stray clouds passed under their wings, soon solidifying into a white carpet, thousands of feet below, that obscured all sight of the earth.

Cherry turned from the window and looked at Bob. "Tell me about this place we're going to," she said.

"I don't know anything about Ngogo itself," he said, "but if it's typical of the other Kikuyu villages I've seen, you aren't going to like it very much at first sight. Native Africa takes a little bit of getting used to."

"Then you've been in Africa before?" Cherry was surprised.

"Yes," Bob replied. "Five years ago Dad took me on a two-month hunting safari in Kenya and Tanganyika as a graduation present when I finished med school. We traveled light—just the two of us, with one white hunter, three boys, a Land Rover and a lorry—and we covered just about all the territory between the Northern Highlands and the Mountains of the Moon. And by the time we got back, we had enough trophies to cover all four walls of Dad's den."

Cherry wrinkled her nose. "I don't think I like the idea," she said, "of killing wild animals just to mount their heads or skins on a wall."

"In those days," Bob explained seriously, "it was necessary to hold the animal population down to an even level so they wouldn't overrun the native farms. The British game commissioners issued just enough hunting licenses to keep the game herds under control."

He thought for a moment.

"But today it's a different story. With most of the British control officers gone, it's hard for the natives to understand why they shouldn't kill all the animals in sight. They even set snares and traps. And a lot of the species are already in danger of becoming extinct. I guess it's just one of the problems involved in teaching an essentially undeveloped people how to learn to govern themselves."

"But they *are* learning, aren't they?" Cherry asked.

"Yes," Bob agreed, "they're learning. But it's a long, slow process. And that is the main reason why we are going to Kenya. To help them learn faster."

He nodded his head to indicate something behind them. "Don't look now," he said, "but did you see that tall fellow, dressed in a chieftain's robe who is carrying a fly whisk?"

"Yes," Cherry said. "What's it for?"

"It's a symbol of dignity," Bob explained. "It's made out of a giraffe's tail."

"A *what?*"

"The tip of a giraffe's tail. Native hunters kill a giraffe, cut off the end of its tail, and leave the rest to the hyenas and buzzards."

Cherry shuddered. "That sounds dreadful."

"To our way of thinking, it is," Bob agreed. "But the natives claim that if it's all right for a white man to kill an animal for its head or its horns or its ivory, it's just as all right for them to kill one for its tail."

Cherry forced a weak smile. "How did we get on this awful subject?"

"I didn't mean to upset you, Cherry," Bob said softly. "But you're going into the real Africa, the bush country. And you might as well have an idea of the problems you're going to have to face. And as to how we got on this subject, you asked me about Ngogo."

"That's better," Cherry said, brightening. "What will it be like?"

"Well, since I've never seen it, I can only tell you what it will probably look like." Bob scratched his chin as he tried to conjure up a picture in his mind. "Ngogo will be a cluster of mud-and-stick huts set down in a clearing in the bush. There will be no telephones—no paved roads—not much civilization at all. The huts will be thatched with coarse, heavy elephant grass, which will undoubtedly be alive with bugs and flies. That's going to be one of our first problems in sanitation, getting rid of the insect population. And when we've done that, we'll have won half the battle in curing the human population."

"I can't wait to get started," Cherry said, excitement in her voice.

"It won't be a Sunday-school picnic," Bob cautioned. "In fact, it'll be real rugged. Even though the Abercrombie Foundation is loaded with money, its work is so widespread that you and I are going to have to rely pretty much on ourselves. But headquarters in

Washington has promised me a couple of young engineers to help us get started."

Suddenly he pointed out the plane window. "Look! There are the Alps!"

Thousands of feet beneath their wings, jutting out of a layer of white clouds, were half a dozen jagged peaks of bare stone, their tips covered with snow like the icing on a cake.

"They're wonderful!" Cherry breathed. "I've never seen anything so lovely in my life!"

"Wait till you see Mount Kilimanjaro," Bob told her. "It's the most beautiful mountain on earth. It rises straight up out of an African plain that is level for hundreds of miles around. And even though it sits almost squarely on the equator, it is snow-capped all the year round just like those peaks you see down there.

"So," he went on, "in spite of the fact that Ngogo is apt to be pretty grim, Africa as a whole is delightful. Along with plenty of work, you'll have a lot of fun. I'll take you on as many side trips as we have time for—and once we get things under control, we'll make a short safari. But we'll be armed with cameras instead of guns."

The Alps had slid quickly out of sight, and the view below became once more an unbroken carpet of clouds, tinted pink by the brilliant rays of the afternoon sun. As the jet sliced silently and effortlessly through the upper reaches of the atmosphere, the motionless feeling of sitting still in space became a sort of soundless lullaby.

Cherry's head was abuzz with more questions about Africa. But, glancing around, she noticed that Bob had been overcome by the curious euphoria of jet flight and had quietly dozed off. So, she saw, had most of the other passengers—including the robed African with the giraffe-tail whisk. She kept looking down at the layer of clouds below.

Then, quite suddenly, the clouds cleared, and below was a broad expanse of water, the surface changing from a deep azure to dark purple in the last of the evening sun. She knew it was the Mediterranean Sea. And beyond the Mediterranean lay Africa! And somewhere in Africa was Ngogo!

It was getting dark when the now-black water of the sea gave way to a broad expanse of desert. The plane began losing altitude, and Cherry could make out a barren landscape of sand, broken here and there by clusters of palm trees that she recognized as oases.

Bob was awake now, and he leaned over from his aisle seat to peer out her window. "This is Egypt," he told her. "We'll be setting down in Cairo pretty soon."

As he spoke, Cherry looked down and gasped. Under the jet's wings was the triangular bulk of the Great Pyramid, flanked by the two lesser ones that stood on either side.

"Oh," she blurted out, "it's just like in the movies!"

Bob beamed. "Your first look at Africa! Didn't I tell you it was something to see?"

Cherry could only stare wordlessly down at the ancient spectacle. Then a sign at the front end of the cabin flashed on:

FASTEN SEAT BELTS
NO SMOKING

Now the plane went into a banking turn, and the blackened concrete of an airstrip rushed up to meet them. With only the slightest screech of tires, the airplane and the earth met again.

"We'll have a two- or three-hour layover here," Bob said. "This jet goes on to Nairobi and South Africa, but it has to wait for planes from feeder lines that come in from Algeria and Arabia. Air transportation in Africa has progressed a long way, but it still isn't what we've come to take for granted back home in the States."

Cherry was fascinated by the crowds they found in the terminal. Cairo, she thought, was like the crossroads of a completely new world. There were swarthy-faced men with white suits and red fezzes; Arabs dressed in tall turbans and long robes that swept the floor as they walked by; a smattering of khaki-clad men who appeared to be government officials; and of course the ever-present quota of tourists who were taking in the strange surroundings with bugged eyes.

"Since we have some time to kill," Bob suggested, "why don't we take a tour around town and then wind up at a native restaurant for dinner?"

"Lead on," Cherry said. "I'm beginning to like this part of the world."

The antique taxi that Bob flagged outside the terminal took them through the modern part of Cairo—down palm-lined avenues that were edged with tall office buildings; past the towering minarets of Moslem mosques; and across the old stone bridges that spanned the Nile. Cherry gasped with delight at the almost endless procession of native feluccas that passed up and down the river, their square lateen sails set to catch every whiff of the evening breeze.

Then, at Bob's direction, the taxi crossed a bridge and turned into a narrow, winding cobbled street that ran along the riverbank. Even though darkness had fallen, the street was crowded, and the open bazaars seemed to be doing a thriving business. At last they pulled up before a narrow, arched doorway, with Arabic characters painted in red curlicue letters over its top.

Inside the small, crowded room, heavy with the aroma of incense and tobacco smoke, a grinning waiter showed them to a corner table.

"I thought," Bob said, "that you might like to have a go at Arabian food. Shall we try the couscous?"

Cherry had been delighted with the whole evening. "I'll try anything," she told him, smiling happily. "But don't I remember from somewhere that you have to eat couscous with your fingers?"

"For a young American lady of fashion, who obviously isn't accustomed to eating with her fingers," Bob said, "I am certain the management will make an exception and bring us knives and forks."

The couscous—an aromatic stew of lamb, vegetables, and tiny dumplings—was delicious. Cherry and Bob lingered over it, and the steaming cups of fragrant mint tea that followed, for more than an hour. Quite naturally, their talk drifted to their coming assignment in Kenya, to the Abercrombie Foundation, the hospital they would have to build in the wilderness, and the problems of transportation and supply.

As they talked, happy and relaxed, Cherry noticed a small, sallow-faced man, sitting at the adjoining table, who seemed to be listening surreptitiously to every word that passed between them. Each time she cast a side glance at him, he was gazing intently into his teacup, but his balding head was cocked slightly as though he had one ear tuned in on them like a radio antenna.

The man's appearance, and his obvious attitude of eavesdropping, gave Cherry an eerie feeling, especially in this little room with its tables crowded so closely together and most of the customers looking like characters out of a cloak-and-dagger movie.

Suddenly she had a sensation that eyes were staring

into her back. She turned abruptly in her chair, and caught the little man in the act of looking directly at her and Bob. At first he quickly lowered his eyes, then he raised them again and gave her a thin smile and a little bow of his head. She turned back to Bob, who had apparently been unaware of this little byplay and was sipping his tea and talking on about Ngogo.

Then the man was standing at their table, his startling white teeth shining through a wide grin.

"Permit me to introduce myself," he said, with a slight trace of an accent that Cherry could not quite place. "I am Spiro Krynos, a trader. The room is so small, and—ah—I could not help overhearing parts of your conversation. May I—ah—would you mind if I joined you and perhaps bought you a pastry?"

Under these odd circumstances there didn't seem to be much that Bob could say except: "Glad to have you. Pull up a chair."

Krynos quickly reached over and got a chair from his table. Bob introduced Cherry and himself, then added, "But I'm afraid that Miss Ames and I wouldn't care for any pastry."

"In that case, I don't either," the little man said.

Cherry thought to herself, "I've never seen anyone so aggressive. I wonder what he really wants."

"I don't mean to be—what do you Americans call it?—nosy?" he said, still grinning his big grin. "But when I accidentally heard you talking about the outbreak of sickness in the Kenya bush south of

Nairobi, and the clinic you are going to build, I naturally became interested. I know that country well, and of course I have long been concerned about the plight of those poor, underprivileged people."

"You say you're a trader, Mr. Krynos?" Bob asked.

"Yes. I deal in sisal and pyrethrum. And I do a lot of business with the Kikuyu farmers in Nairobi." He shrugged his shoulders. "I hesitate to appear mercenary—but, ah, illness among the native farmers would badly hurt my business." Then he hastily added, "You understand, of course, that my first concern is for the people themselves."

"Sure, sure," Bob said. "We understand."

Cherry saw that Bob, too, was getting a little annoyed. But her inborn curiosity made her want to hear more about what Krynos had on his mind. He certainly didn't look like a man who would go out of his way to strike up an acquaintance in a crowded Cairo café.

"Sisal," she said. "I know about that. Rope is made out of its fiber. But what is this py-pyre-?"

"Pyrethrum," Bob volunteered. "It's a pretty flower that African farmers grow as a crop. Its seed is processed into an insecticide."

"Well"—Cherry laughed—"maybe we are going to need a lot of it when we go to work on the flies and bugs in Ngogo."

"So Ngogo is where your clinic is going to be?" said

Mr. Krynos. "I've been there many times. It's a rather obscure little village, about fifty miles south of Nairobi. The natives raise lots of pyrethrum. I'm sorry to hear that its people are in trouble."

"We're going to do all we can to get rid of the trouble," Bob said. "I don't suppose there's a doctor nearer than Nairobi."

"I'm afraid not," Mr. Krynos said, shaking his head. "Oh, now and then a government doctor drives down from the city. But there are so many people—and so few qualified doctors. A pity. But those conditions are all too common in the newly developing countries." He pulled out a silk handkerchief and delicately swabbed his damp forehead. "Again excuse my inquisitiveness, and my involuntary eavesdropping. But it isn't often that I have a chance to talk with intelligent young Americans. Didn't you say that your work was being sponsored by a private American organization?"

"Yes," Bob replied. "The Abercrombie Foundation." Then, warming up to the subject nearest to his heart, he explained all about the Foundation's work, the clinic they were going to build, and what they hoped to accomplish.

For nearly all of the next hour Cherry listened as the two men talked. She noticed particularly that the little man kept asking pointed questions about the details of their setup. And Bob, eager to talk about the project, answered them all and supplied some additional information of his own.

The waiter brought more mint tea, and the men went on talking, Cherry contributing a word here and there, but for the most part keeping silent and listening.

One puzzling thought kept running through her head. *Why should an itinerant trader suddenly be so interested in a health program he has never heard of before?*

Suddenly Bob looked at his watch. "I'm afraid," he said, "that Miss Ames and I had better be getting back to the airport. This has been most interesting and pleasant, but if you will excuse us, we must return to the airport now."

Mr. Krynos snapped his fingers. "And I," he said, "have forgotten an important telephone call that I should have made an hour ago."

He motioned to the waiter, and, despite Bob's protest, insisted on paying their check. "At least I owe you that much"—he beamed—"for the pleasantest evening I have had in months."

Plucking a wallet from his inside jacket pocket, he extracted a bill of large denomination and grandly waved the waiter away with instructions to keep the change. Whereupon, he arose and bowed to Cherry.

"It has been a great pleasure," he said. And once more his white teeth glistened in a wide grin. "*Au revoir!* And may we meet again!"

And with that he turned on his heels and vanished into the crowded room.

"He turned out to be a nice guy," Bob said. "Interested in everything."

"Maybe," Cherry replied. "But he was trying his best to quiz us. I wonder why he would want to do that."

Bob laughed at the puzzled expression on her face. "Oh, now, come off it, Cherry. You've seen too many Grade-B spy thrillers. He's just interested in the people down in Kenya. After all, as he said, he makes his living trading with them. And besides, he probably doesn't often get a chance to spend an evening with a pretty American girl. Now we'd better 'git' if we don't want that plane to leave without us."

Cherry reached for her bag, and as she did so, she saw a folded piece of white paper on the floor underneath the table.

"What's this?" she said, picking it up.

Bob took it from her and smoothed it out. It was a telegram sent from Nairobi and addressed to Mr. Spiro Krynos.

"It must have fallen out of his wallet when he reached for his money," Bob suggested.

He read the wire, then gave it to Cherry.

"I guess it has to do with a business deal," he said. "So since he's read it, it can't be too important if he's lost it."

Cherry's brows wrinkled as she read the telegram:

MZABITE FAILED TO DELIVER. ORDER STOPPED.

SMITH

Mzabite! That was an odd name!

"Let's go," Bob said. "We may have a problem getting a taxi in this part of town. I'll leave this wire with the cashier in case Krynos needs it and comes back here looking for it."

CHAPTER III

Nairobi

WHEN CHERRY AND BOB REACHED THE CAIRO AIR-port, they discovered that their flight had been unex-pectedly delayed for another two hours. Cherry was exhausted when they finally got aboard and found their seats again. She had hardly settled down and leaned back against the headrest before she fell into a sound sleep.

The brilliant rays of the early-morning sun, slant-ing in through the plane's window, gently nudged her awake. Looking out, she saw that the jet was appar-ently losing altitude for a landing. Below them was a range of low, bush-covered hills. Away off in the distance, she could make out the deep-purple ridges of a higher mountain chain. Then the hills began to level off into a broad, grass-covered plain, with small groves of curiously flat-topped trees scattered here and there at random. As she watched, a large herd of gazelles bounded off across the grass in long, leaping strides.

"Oh, look, Bob!" Cherry said, coming fully awake now. "Aren't they the cutest things you ever saw?"

"Thomson's gazelles," Bob told her. "The commonest antelope in the bush. No matter how much they're hunted, they seem to thrive and multiply. They are the standard meat dish of most safaris."

No sooner had the plane passed over the gazelle herd, than half a dozen giraffes appeared, loping along in their awkward stiff-legged canter.

Cherry was too excited to talk. She just pointed at them.

"We are coming in over Nairobi National Park," Bob said. "Maybe this afternoon, after we have gotten organized, I'll drive you out and you can see all the animals close up."

The people at Eastleigh Airport in Nairobi were even more varied and interesting than those Cherry had seen in Cairo. It was easy to tell the difference between those who were leaving and those who were just arriving. The former, their faces burned bright red or deep tan from the merciless East African sun, were wearing faded safari clothes—a mark of distinction, Cherry thought. The new arrivals were pale of face, and looking about them curiously, as Cherry was doing now. Luggage was piled all over the waiting room, and native porters in white shorts and white jackets moved about carrying great loads of baggage.

As Bob and Cherry stood patiently in line to have their cases examined by the customs officials, a tall, middle-aged, swarthy man wearing a faded and wrinkled bush jacket and a battered felt hat passed by and eyed Bob curiously. Then he came over and stuck out his hand.

"Aren't you young Bob Barton?" the man asked in a clipped British accent. "Didn't I take you and your father on safari three or four years ago?"

Bob shook the big hand and smiled. "Hi, Jack! I'm surprised you remembered me."

"I never forget a client." The big man grinned. "You and your wife here for another hunt?"

Bob introduced Cherry and explained their business. "This is Long Jack Robertson," he told her. "The best white hunter in the business."

"Thanks for those kind words," Long Jack said. "So you're a doctor now! And going down to Ngogo! I heard there was some kind of sickness there, but I haven't been down that way for quite a while." He scratched the graying stubble on his square chin. "The safari business," he said, "isn't what it used to be. Game's scarce, and people don't seem to want to rough it any more like you and your daddy did. About all I ever shoot nowadays is a Tommie or two for the pot."

"What are you doing out here at the airport, Jack?" Bob asked. "Meeting a client?"

"No, I'm just seeing a party off. But I've got another one coming in a day or so."

Just then the customs man motioned to Bob and Cherry that they were next.

"We'll stay at the New Stanley overnight," Bob said. "Drop around this evening, and maybe we'll buy you a dinner."

"Good deal," Long Jack replied.

It was still midmorning when Cherry and Bob checked in at the New Stanley. Then they met on the hotel veranda for a cup of tea.

When they had finished, Bob said, "I just tried to call Mr. Gikingu—he's the Abercrombie Foundation's representative here in Kenya. But his office says he's out of town. So let's go get ourselves outfitted, unless you're tired and want to take a nap."

Cherry looked out on the busy street. The sidewalks were crowded with people hurrying along in the blazing sunlight. Arabs, Turks, Europeans—and a few rugged-looking, mahogany-tanned men, whose bush jackets were clean, but faded and bleached from many washings. These latter, she thought, must be professional guides and white hunters like Long Jack Robertson.

"I'm much too excited about being in Africa to want a nap," Cherry declared. "Let's go get outfitted."

Their first stop was a small clothing shop on a side

street. Inside, it was almost dark compared to the glaring sun of the outdoors.

"I told you," Bob said, "that you'd have no use for nice white nurses' uniforms. So here is where we get suited up."

A small, dark-skinned man came over and bowed slightly. "May I help you, sir and madam?"

At Bob's suggestion, Cherry ordered three pairs of khaki slacks, three khaki skirts, and three khaki bush jackets, a dozen pairs of light cotton socks, and two pairs of ankle-high boots. Then Bob ordered comparable outfits for himself. When Bob paid the bill with a traveler's check, the proprietor of the shop bowed again.

"Send those things over to the New Stanley," Bob told him. And they went out again into the bright sunlight.

"The nice thing about being a rich man's son," Bob said as they walked down the street, "is that you don't have to wait for expense vouchers to clear through the red tape in Washington. So I am going to buy us a car. We'll ride now, and Abercrombie will pay later."

At the next corner was an automobile agency with a shiny, new olive-drab Land Rover in the showroom window. They went in.

"Take that one outside and gas it up," Bob said to the salesman, reaching for his traveler's checkbook. "And where can I get a good, strong two-way radio?"

"We have them here, sir," the clerk said.

"Fine," Bob told him. "Send your best model to me at the New Stanley."

When their new Land Rover, serviced and ready to roll, pulled up at the curb, Bob handed Cherry into the seat.

"Now," he said, "I promised to show you some animals. So off we go."

Ten minutes later they were leaving the city behind and driving out into an open plain. At scattered intervals, groves of flat-topped acacia trees gave the landscape the typically African look that Cherry knew so well from adventure movies.

"This is Nairobi National Game Park, only four miles from the city," Bob explained. "It's an unfenced zoo. The animals live here just as they do in the wildest parts of the bush, but nobody bothers them. They have a pretty soft life."

As Cherry watched, a herd of a dozen or so zebras came into view. Grazing among them, occasionally lifting their long necks into the air as if scenting the breeze, were three or four giraffes.

"The zebras like to have giraffes for company," Bob said. "They're good lookouts. They can see lions coming from a long way off, and when they run, the zebras run too."

"But how about those lions over there?" Cherry asked, her voice filled with excitement. She pointed to a pride of lions—two black-maned males and a dozen

The lions were dozing in the noonday sun

females—that were dozing in the noonday sun. "The zebras don't seem to be afraid of them."

"Lions don't kill unless they are hungry," Bob told her. "And zebras seem to know the difference. Don't ask me why. But they can tell a hungry lion from a well-fed one."

Cherry was puzzled. "Isn't it dangerous to have wild lions wandering around so close to town?"

"Not generally," Bob said. "Oh, once in a great while one strays into the suburbs. But they're more afraid of people than people are of them. There's no such thing as a man-eater around here. And anyhow, there are enough zebras and antelopes to keep them well-fed and happy. As I told you, this park is like the wild bush. The grass-eaters eat the grass, and the lions eat the grass-eaters. The only unnatural law that applies here affects people. You're not allowed to get out of your car."

All afternoon Cherry and Bob drove along the park's roads. They passed a number of other tourists' cars, and several sightseeing buses. Then, as the red ball of sun was settling down behind the mountains to the west, Bob headed back for Nairobi.

Sitting with Bob on the broad hotel veranda in the cool of the evening, drinking lemonade out of a tall ice-filled glass, Cherry noticed a balding, middle-aged man, with two professional-looking cameras hanging around his neck, closely studying all the guests. To her surprise, he came over to their table and introduced himself.

"Excuse me," the man started out. "My name is Ed Smith and I'm here in Nairobi on assignment from *Click* magazine in New York, just picking up local color. You folks appear to be on your honeymoon, and I wondered if you would let me take your picture and give me a short interview."

Cherry blushed to the roots of her black hair, and Bob roared with laughter.

"This is the second time today we've been taken for married people, Cherry."

"I beg your pardon," the man said, apparently embarrassed.

"Sorry," Bob said. "I'm Dr. Barton and this is my nurse, Miss Ames. We are here in Kenya strictly on business."

"Oh, yes," Mr. Smith said, brightening. "I should have known. I read about you in today's paper."

"In the *paper?*"

Smith pointed to a copy of the *Nairobi News* that had been placed on the tray with their glasses of lemonade. "There is a story about your arrival in town. You're with the Abercrombie Foundation, aren't you?"

"Yes," Bob said. "But I'm surprised that we made the paper. Won't you sit down for a moment and join us in a lemonade?"

"Don't mind if I do," Smith said. "It's a hot

evening." He sat down and unwound the camera straps from his neck, placing them on the back of the chair.

"Speaking of *Click*," Cherry volunteered, "I've met George Young. One day last winter my brother Charlie took me to lunch with him in New York."

"George *who?*" Mr. Smith said, his forehead wrinkling in puzzlement.

"George Young," Cherry repeated. "Isn't he the picture editor of *Click?*"

"Oh, sure. Good old George," Smith said. "Finest editor in New York." He took a sip of the lemonade the waiter had brought him. "Ah-h! Nothing like a cold drink to take the edge off a warm day."

"Now that's strange," Cherry thought. "A photographer from *Click* who doesn't recognize the name George Young!" She had an overpowering hunch. "And Hank Bloom was there too," she added. "He and my brother Charlie went to college together. He's the assistant editor, isn't he?"

"He sure is," Ed Smith replied heartily. "He snaps the whip on us poor photographers every hour on the hour."

"What a phony!" Cherry said to herself. Hank Bloom was a name that she had made up on the spur of the moment! She made a mental note to talk about this to Bob. But for the life of her she couldn't see why a photographer like this Ed Smith should be in Nairobi flying false colors. Then she remembered what Bob had said last night in Cairo. Maybe she *had* been seeing too many Grade-B spy movies. And, of all places, Nairobi was the perfect stage setting!

Just then Long Jack Robertson came sauntering along the veranda. He was dressed in spanking clean, stiffly starched khakis, and he carried a riding crop under his left arm.

"Cheers, folks," he said. "I won't be able to have dinner with you, but I've got a minute or two to have a chat."

Bob made the introductions, and Smith and Robertson shook hands in the stiff manner that strangers often do. Smith collected his cameras from the back of the chair and arose to go.

"I'd better be running along," he said. "Maybe I'll see you around."

"Odd duck," Long Jack said when Smith had gone. "But then we get all kinds here in Kenya. Glad to see that you're looking so fit, Bob. How's your dad, by the way?"

For a while Bob and the hunter swapped stories about their safari, as Cherry listened. Then Robertson noticed the newspaper on the tray.

"I see you've got the *News* here. Did you read the story about my client?"

"I haven't had a chance to see the paper yet," Bob replied, "although I understand that my name is in it. What's all this about your client?"

Long Jack grinned. "I'll never hear the last of it if

I live to be a hundred. This character had made reservations for a hunting safari. But when we got out in the bush, hunting seemed to be the last thing on his mind. He spent all his time loafing around camp, reading and snoozing. And it didn't take me long to find out that he hardly knew which end of a gun fired the bullet.

"Anyway," Long Jack continued, "one day he suggested that it wouldn't do for him to go back to England without some kind of trophy to show his friends—and how would I like to go out and bag him one or two? So I took my number-one boy, Jimmo—you remember him, Bob, he was with me when I took out you and your dad—and we had the jolly good luck to kick up a prime sable antelope and a better-than-average kudu. They seemed to satisfy my client to the nines, and the next morning we broke camp and safaried back here to Nairobi."

"Well," Bob said, "I guess it isn't unusual for a man to make a safari, have his hunter shoot the game, and then hang his trophies on the wall of his living room and brag about them all the rest of his life."

"Yes, that's so," Long Jack agreed. "But there apparently was more to this character than met the eye. When we got back here, he asked me to take the heads to old Ali Hadj, the Mzabite taxidermist, to be mounted, and . . ."

Cherry, who had been listening with only half an ear to the men's hunting talk, suddenly perked up and took notice. There was that word again—the one in Kyrnos' telegram. Mzabite!

"What's a Mzabite?" she asked eagerly.

"Well," Jack said, "Mzabites are a desert tribe that live in the middle of the Sahara. But instead of being nomadic herdsmen, like most Arabs, they are a merchant people. Their young men go out to all the cities of Africa, and even southern Europe, and set themselves up as merchants and traders. A young Mzabite may be gone from his home for as long as twenty-five or thirty years. And by the time he returns—they always go back to their homeland in their old age—he has made his fortune. Then his son, or another young man from his village, goes to take over the business." Long Jack shrugged. "They're unusual types, no getting around that.

"Anyhow," Long Jack went on, "my client left his heads with the Mzabite, with instructions to have the trophies air-expressed to him in London. Then my client paid his bill, took off for England, and that's the last I heard of him—until this morning."

"You're making it sound like a real mystery, Mr. Robertson," Cherry said.

"Well, it was," the hunter said. "Something made the customs people up in London suspicious—I still don't know all the details. But for some reason or other they examined the heads closely, and found that the antelope's horns were filled with a small fortune in uncut diamonds."

Bob whistled. "Whew! Rough diamonds in Nairobi!"

"A real puzzler," the hunter said. "But apparently the Mzabite had gotten the word, and by the time the police went around to pick him up, he had disappeared. Probably scooted back into the Sahara where he'd be as hard to find as a particular grain of sand."

Like a blinding light, the words of the telegram she and Bob had seen in the Cairo café flashed through Cherry's head. How did they go? "Mzabite failed to deliver. Order stopped." Yes, that was it! Could there be a connection somewhere? It seemed preposterous. And yet . . .

When her whirling thoughts came back to the present, Long Jack was still talking.

"Of course the local constabulary questioned me, and even though I couldn't tell them much, I got into the papers as the hunter who had bagged the sable in the first place."

"Well, Jack"—Bob laughed—"it will be good advertising for you. All your clients will expect you to find them trophies full of diamonds."

"I can do without that kind of publicity," Long Jack said, smiling wryly. "I'll be guyed about it for years."

Bob looked at his watch.

"Cherry," he said, "you and I had better start thinking about dinner. I expect you'll want to powder your nose and freshen your lipstick." He turned to the hunter. "Are you sure you won't join us, Jack?"

"Thanks, no," Robertson said, getting to his feet. "I'm taking out my party in a couple of days and I've got some arrangements to make. But thank heaven these are people who want a camera safari. No mounted heads this trip."

Half an hour later, Cherry stepped from the old-fashioned hotel elevator on the way down from her room to join Bob in the restaurant. There was the usual dinner-hour gathering in the lobby—the mixed assortment of Arabs, African Negroes, and Europeans that is so typical of post-independence Kenya.

As she made her way through the crowd, she caught sight of a familiar figure out of the corner of her eye. Standing under a potted palm at the side of the room was the tall figure of Long Jack Robertson, and he was talking intimately and nervously to— Why, the second man was Ed Smith, the photographer.

Taking care not to look directly at them, Cherry stopped, took her compact from her bag, and pretended to touch up her lipstick. The little mirror afforded a perfect view—a clear reflection of Robertson and Smith engaged in deep conversation. Putting her compact away, she went on to the dining room where Bob was waiting at the door.

A headwaiter showed them to their table, and they were just starting in on the soup course when the photographer appeared and said hello. Bob asked him to join them.

"Sorry," Smith said. "I have another appointment. But since talking to you folks a while ago, I've had what I think may be a great idea."

Both Cherry and Bob looked quizzically at him.

"It occurred to me," Smith went on, "that I might get a whale of a picture story at this clinic you two are setting up. Place called Ngogo, didn't the news item say?"

Bob nodded.

"Well, it struck me that if I should drive down there after I've finished my assignment here in Nairobi—and of course if you don't mind—I might get some interesting sidelights about what Americans are doing to help the people of the new African nations."

"Not bad," Bob agreed. "Not a bad idea at all. And it ought to be good publicity for the Foundation. What do you think, Cherry?"

"Yes, it should," Cherry said. But she was really thinking that it might give her a chance to see something more of this mysterious Ed Smith, the magazine photographer who didn't even know his own editors.

"Then fine," Smith said, getting up. "I'll be popping in on you one of these days soon."

CHAPTER IV

Ngogo

BY MIDMORNING THE NEXT DAY CHERRY AND
young Bob Barton were bouncing along a rough dirt
road—little more than a wide trail—southward from
Nairobi to Ngogo. Both were dressed in their spanking new safari clothes, and Cherry was grateful for
the wide-brimmed felt hat that protected her face and
the back of her neck from the blazing rays of the sun.
A bright silk kerchief was knotted about her neck,
and she wore dark sunglasses.

All of their gear, including the new two-way radio,
was neatly stowed in the back of the Land Rover. Bob
had surprised her when he had included two gun
cases.

"Are we going to need *guns?*" she had asked, a little
uneasily.

"Not for the reasons you might be thinking of,"
Bob reassured her. "One of these is a 20-gauge

shotgun and the other is a .30–06 sporting rifle. The shotgun I'll use to bag us a few sand grouse every now and then. There are millions of them down in this part of Kenya, and when they're broiled over an open fire they taste ten times better than the partridge or pheasants your twin brother probably hunts every fall back in Illinois. And compared to a brace of sand grouse, a Thanksgiving turkey hardly seems fit to eat.

"Now with the rifle, I'll go out into Nature's great supermarket once in a while and bring home an occasional antelope steak. Before our assignment here is finished, my girl, you're going to welcome a change of pace in the menu." He laughed. "So don't let the guns worry you."

Cherry glanced at Bob as he sat behind the wheel of the Land Rover. The thought occurred to her that, at the moment, he looked more like a professional white hunter than a doctor. Odd—but she had never realized before just how really handsome he was. He was tall and straight and trim in his open-necked bush jacket. And the deep brown of his face and forearms, nearly as dark as that of Long Jack Robertson, was accentuated by his light-blond hair.

"How did you get such a good tan working in a hospital in Washington?" Cherry found herself saying.

Bob laughed. "Well, we research doctors don't exactly stay holed up in a lab twenty-four hours a day.

And the summer sun at the Rock Creek golf course
can get almost as hot as it does here on the equator."

"Well, I'm glad I brought along a good supply of
suntan cream," Cherry said brightly. "I don't tan. I
burn."

"In Africa," Bob informed her, "you'll soon tan."

They drove along for a time in silence, looking out
at the broad grassy plains and the occasional herds of
antelopes that scampered by in the distance. All the
while, Cherry's mind kept churning over the puzzling
happenings of the past couple of days.

"Look, Bob," she said at last, "I've got a funny
feeling."

Bob slammed on the brakes, and looked at her
closely as the car skidded to a stop.

"It's probably the sun," he said anxiously. "I'll pull
over into the next stand of trees we see, and you can
rest a while in the shade." He took a Thermos of cold
water out of the door compartment. "Here," he told
her. "Take a pull at this."

Cherry had to laugh. "No, it's not that kind of
funny. I'm not going to faint from the heat. It's all the
peculiar things that have been going on ever since we
came to Africa."

"Well, that's a relief," Bob said. "Peculiar things
like what?"

"To begin with," Cherry began, "there was that
night in Cairo."

First she recalled to him the telegram that had apparently fallen out of Spiro Krynos' wallet, and the cryptic message it contained, and the fact that it had been signed "Smith"—then Ed Smith, the photographer, who didn't recognize the name of the editor of *Click,* but who had quickly pretended to know the nonexistent Hank Bloom—then the attempt to smuggle diamonds out of Kenya in the horns of a mounted antelope head—and finally the earnest conversation she had observed in the hotel lobby between Smith and the white hunter.

"What I meant," she finished, "is that it all gives me a funny feeling that something queer is going on right under our noses."

Bob thought about it for a minute, then he said, "Cherry, they don't call Africa the 'Dark Continent' or the 'Land of Mystery' for nothing. Something happens to people when they first come here. I don't know what it is, but I know what it feels like. Maybe it's compounded of the smell of elephant grass browning in the sun, and the sweet scent of mimosa in the hedgerows. Or the sight of zebras and antelope ranging wild across the bush. Or the strange people and their strange customs. Or, perhaps most of all, the fact that primitive Africa is only just emerging from the Stone Age. It's all different from anything you've ever been used to."

He took a pipe from his pocket, filled it, and lighted

it up. "I'm not saying that your imagination is running away with you," he went on. "But let's look at these things one at a time. First, the Mzabites are the merchant class of Africa. There are thousands of them, and they have shops and stores from Algiers to Zanzibar and everywhere in between. Second, Smith is the commonest name in the English language.

"Now about the photographer and Long Jack. Smith had just learned from us that Jack was a professional white hunter, and he was more than likely sounding him out for a story possibility. Nothing unusual about that. And as for Smith himself, he's probably a free-lancer, hoping to sell some African stories to the magazine. So he was putting up a big front with us, pretending to be on friendly terms with editors that he actually doesn't even know."

Bob leaned back in the seat, took a long puff on his pipe, and gave Cherry a brotherly smile. "So— poof!—there goes your mystery floating away in a cloud of romance."

Cherry still wasn't satisfied. "But how about the diamonds in the antelope's head?"

"Look!" Bob said. "If I had a dollar for every diamond plot ever hatched in Africa I'd be richer than my dad. And besides, what could all this skulduggery you're dreaming up possibly have to do with us?"

Cherry couldn't answer the question.

"O.K.," Bob said. "Let's get on down this trail and

see what our future home looks like." He stepped on the starter and the Land Rover jounced ahead over the ruts in the dry dirt road.

When they were well outside the suburbs of Nairobi, they began passing by isolated farms. For the most part, these farms consisted of patches of banana trees, fields of stunted corn, and broad expanses of golden flowers that looked something like the Queen Anne's lace that grew wild back in Illinois. A few men, wearing faded khaki pants and nothing from the waist up, were working among the rows of corn.

"You asked me about pyrethrum the other night," Bob said, indicating the flowers that were blowing slightly in the faint breeze. "There it is. When it's ripe, the native farmers cut it, hang it up in bunches to dry, and then sell it to traders like that man we saw in Cairo."

"But I don't see any houses," Cherry said. "Where do the farmers live?"

"They all live together in little villages like the one we're going to." He glanced at the mileage indicator on the dashboard. "In fact, I'd say that we're only about half a mile or so from Ngogo right now, and that's probably where these people live. They walk back and forth every day."

"I would think they'd have farms closer to their homes," Cherry said.

"Well, they don't actually own the land," Bob went on. "The soil here is rich, but it wears out quickly. And when it does, the farmers simply move to another location. Of course it's different up north where the white settlers made big plantations. There they employ modern farming methods—crop rotation, and the like. But the Kikuyus have been farming like this for centuries, and it seems to supply their needs." He pointed to a cluster of huts that had come into view up ahead. "Unless I miss my guess, we're coming to Ngogo now."

The village of Ngogo was just about the way Bob had pictured it—a circular clearing in the midst of the bush. Native huts, made of dried mud plastered over stick frameworks, ringed the outer edges of the clearing. The clearing itself was hard-packed earth, and in the center was a large fireplace, which was no more than a ring of smoke-blackened stones on the ground. A narrow, crystal-clear stream wound past the settlement; and in the river's bend, sheltered by a grove of acacia trees, a new large wooden building was almost completed.

At the approach of the Land Rover, several half-naked children who had been playing in the clearing streaked for the shelter of the huts. And a dozen or so scrawny chickens flapped screeching into the surrounding bush. A few women stood in the narrow doorways.

Bob drove across the compound toward the new building, where a number of native workmen were putting the finishing touches on a roof. Working with them was a tall, slender, deeply tanned young white man.

"Hi, there!" The young man sang out in a distinctly American accent, and he climbed down from the ladder on which he had been working.

Striding up to the car, he took off a floppy canvas hat, wiped the sweaty palm of his hand on his khaki shorts, and extended it in welcome.

"I'm Jeff Jordan," he said, a grin splitting his face. "I guess you're the new doctor."

"Right. Bob Barton. And this is my nurse, Cherry Ames."

"Well, welcome to Ngogo," Jeff said. "My partner and I—he's Chuck Warner, and he drove in to town this morning for supplies—came here ten days ago to build your new hospital." He gestured toward the building with a wave of his hand. "It's almost finished. How does it look to you?"

The clinic was a one-story affair, elevated on heavy six-by-six stilts about three feet off the ground. It had boarded sides up to a height of some five feet, and from there to the roof its sides were of very fine wire screen. Broad wooden steps led up to the screen-door entrance.

"We're making wooden shutters that we can put up over the screens when it rains," Jeff explained.

"It looks great," Bob said. "I hadn't thought that you'd be this far along."

"Well, it was lucky timing," Jeff said. "Chuck and I

had just finished supervising a barracks job at East-leigh Field in Nairobi and were ready to high-tail it home to the States. Then Mr. Gikingu—your Abercrombie Foundation official in Nairobi—got in touch with us and offered us this contract. So we got right on it."

"Good." Bob nodded. "I tried to reach Tom Gikingu by telephone yesterday, but he's out of town. Some sort of emergency or other. So I'll have to wait and see him the next time I'm in Nairobi. Meanwhile, I thought Miss Ames and I had better come on out here and see what things were like."

"What *are* things like, Mr. Jordan?" Cherry asked anxiously. "Among the town people, I mean."

"First off, my name is Jeff. But to answer your question, Miss Ames . . ."

"And *my* name," Cherry said, smiling, "is Cherry."

"O.K., Cherry," Jeff continued, "from what I can see, things aren't any too good. Half the people in the village are down with this sleeping sickness thing. But Chuck and I figured the most useful thing we could do about it was to get this hospital up as fast as we could—and hope for you and the doctor to get here quick."

"Well, we're here now," Bob said as he helped Cherry out of the car. "And we're ready to go to work. But before we look at any of the cases, I think we had better go over your installation, Jeff, and see what we've got to work with."

"In the first place, when we were at the Abercrombie Foundation in Nairobi, Tom Gikingu didn't give us any plans to go on, Doc," Jeff Jordan explained. "If you don't mind my saying so, things aren't very well organized here in Kenya yet—what with the new government taking over and all. So Chuck and I just started from scratch and played it by ear." He stopped and thought a moment. "But Tom Gikingu seems like a nice guy."

"Well," Bob said, "I haven't met Gikingu, but I understand that he is a very capable person. Educated at Oxford University. And the Foundation likes to work with local people whenever it's possible."

Jeff nodded. "I'll say this for Gikingu," he said. "He gave us everything we asked for. We told him what we needed in the way of lumber and machinery, and it was here in the next couple of days. But let's go and look the place over."

The main part of the hospital was one big room, floored with pine boards.

"There ought to be space here," Bob said, "for about fifty beds."

"That's what Chuck and I figured," Jeff Jordan said. "But instead of beds, the best Gikingu could do was send us canvas army cots. We have fifty of 'em under a tarp out in the back. He also sent bed linen, blankets, and towels."

"Good," Bob said. "We'll start setting things up this evening."

"And back here," Jeff said, leading the way, "are four small rooms that we sort of figured you might need for living quarters."

"You guys must have had a crystal ball." Bob beamed. "We'll turn one into a lab. And the other three will be rooms for Cherry, the student nurses, and me. But what are you and your partner doing for living space?"

"Oh, we've got a pair of safari tents down by the river that do us just fine," Jeff said. "Now let's take a look at the rest of the installation and see if you want any changes."

In the rear of the hospital, Jeff showed them a big generator, run by a gasoline motor.

"We've put in a temporary pumping and lighting system," the engineer explained, looking a little proud of himself. "Most of the piping and wiring has already been installed, and by this time tomorrow we'll have running water and electric lights. We ran a line to the river just above this bend, and our tests indicate that the water is good and pure. But just to be on the safe side, we ordered a filter system that Chuck should be bringing from town this afternoon."

"Well, I must say," Bob said, "that you fellows have done a bang-up job, and it's going to make my work—and Cherry's—a whole lot easier." He glanced over at the Kikuyu workmen who were nailing on the roof. "How soon will that roof be finished?"

"Another hour or so," Jeff replied.

"O.K.," Bob said. "When they are through, have your people start scrubbing up the place. Then they can set up the cots. Meanwhile, Miss Ames and I will begin looking in on some of the sleeping sickness cases."

A truck rumbled into the clearing, driven by the second American engineer, Chuck Warner. In the seat beside him were two dark-skinned Kikuyu girls—in their early twenties, Cherry guessed.

"Here's my partner now," Jeff said. "And it looks like he's got a truckload."

Chuck Warner was several inches shorter than either Jeff or Bob, chunky and heavy in the shoulders like a college fullback—and with a head of flaming red hair. When Jeff introduced him, he said, in a soft Southern drawl, "We sure are mighty glad to see you folks. A hospital's no good without doctors and nurses. And speaking of nurses"—he motioned the two native girls to get down out of the truck—"I've got a couple of them here to help you, Miss Cherry. Mr. Gikingu, at the Abercrombie Foundation office in Nairobi, sent 'em to us."

Cherry smiled and said hello.

The girls approached the group timidly. Both wore white coveralls, with red scarves tied over their hair and canvas sneakers on their feet. The taller of the two spoke first, in an accent that seemed to Cherry sort of mission-school English.

"I am Kavarondi. And this is my friend Sara. We have had a year's training at Nairobi General Hospital. Do you think we know enough nursing to help you?"

Sara said shyly, "We volunteered to come here because we know about the epidemic and—and we want to learn from American registered nurse."

Cherry shook hands with Kavarondi, then with Sara. "I can't tell you how happy I am to have your help! A year's training is a good deal, and I'll try to teach you. You'll have to teach me, too, as we work, since I am new to the ways of your country."

Kavarondi, Cherry thought to herself, was an exceptionally handsome young woman. Her skin was a rich, deep color; her features were more Caucasian than African. Her lips were thin; her cheekbones were high, and her hair, while glistening black, was fine and straight. Cherry remembered the old story of the little band of Crusaders that had gotten lost, hundreds of years ago, wandered south from the Holy Land and intermarried with native tribes. She wondered if one of Kavarondi's long-ago grandfathers might have carried a sword and shield in the English Army of Richard the Lion-Hearted. The girl stood tall and straight in her white coveralls. Cherry decided that she would suggest that the girls wear khaki uniforms similar to her own.

Sara, Cherry noted, was quite opposite, unmistakably African; although, unlike most Kikuyu women, she was short and inclined toward stoutness. The lobes of her ears had been pierced in the Kikuyu fashion—when she was a child, Cherry assumed—then had been distended by wooden plugs. Her English was almost as good as Kavarondi's.

Both the Kikuyu girls looked at Cherry with their hearts in their eyes, and she understood how deeply they wanted to serve their people. She was touched. Cherry could remember how the same strong motive had drawn her into nursing—and kept her at it, brought her to the jungle, here, now.

"I'm awfully lucky to have you to help me," she said. "I want you to call me Cherry."

"We are glad you have come here, Cherry," Kavarondi said. "Sister Cherry."

"Cherry. That is a nice name," said Sara, grinning broadly.

Bob Barton smiled at the girls, and picked up the medical bag that he had carried from the Land Rover. "We might as well get to work," he said. "Let's see just what we're up against."

He led the way toward the nearest hut. Cherry and the two native girls followed the young doctor.

What they were up against, Cherry soon discovered, was pretty grim indeed.

The first hut they entered was dark and gloomy inside, with a strong smell of human bodies in the fetid air. The floor was nothing but tamped-down earth, and there was no furniture except a low, crude table and three or four wooden stools. At one side of the hut three people lay on crude pallets of woven grass which were covered by animal skins. Their bodies glistened with oily sweat. One was a man, one a woman, and the third figure was that of a child. A slim, gangling girl of about twelve was kneeling beside the little boy, mopping his face with a damp cloth which she dipped from time to time in a gourd of water. When she saw her visitors, she jumped to her feet, her eyes gleaming with fear.

Kavarondi spoke with her in Swahili. Then she translated.

"She says," Kavarondi reported, "that her father and mother have been sick like this for two weeks, lying as though they were in the long sleep. Her little brother became ill only a few days ago. But now he too is in the long sleep."

Bob bent down over the three of them in turn, and touched his fingers to their foreheads.

"No fever," he said gravely. "Well, I'm not surprised. In these cases it comes and goes intermittently, and never gets very high. There isn't a thing we can do until we get these people into the clinic where we can give them a good washing and proper medication. Then we'll see. Now let's go on and look at the others."

Bob, Cherry, Kavarondi, and Sara visited all of the native houses in turn. As Jeff had said, about half the population was afflicted with the disease. The other half, including the workmen Jeff and Chuck had enlisted, appeared to be normally healthy and happy.

"That's the way this thing strikes," Bob explained. "Like lightning. It hits some people and misses others. All of these Ngogo folks must surely have been fly-bitten at one time or another. I guess the ones that didn't come down must have had their own built-in immunity."

It was growing dark by the time they completed their rounds. "First thing tomorrow," Bob said, "we'll start moving these cases into the hospital. Then we'll begin their treatments."

Cherry said, "I wish we could begin tonight. But of course tonight we have to get the hospital ready. How slow! I could explode!"

Bob gave her an indulgent smile. "There was once a great Greek doctor, named Hippocrates, who said that the science of medicine is compounded largely of the art of patience. If there were any emergency treatments we could give this evening, we'd do it. I don't like waiting overnight, either, Cherry. But the boys say that by tomorrow morning we will have lights and water. We can't give treatments without proper tools."

When they got back to the hospital building, Cherry found that all fifty cots had been installed in orderly rows.

"And we fixed up rough quarters for you and Miss Cherry," Chuck said to Bob. "Tomi—he's our

cook—has some antelope steaks broiling over the fire.
How many of us for supper?"

Kavarondi had an uncle in the village—fortunately
his family had escaped the sickness—and she and Sara
were having supper and spending the night in their
hut. So, an hour later, the four young Americans were
resting in canvas chairs in front of the hospital steps.
The antelope steaks had been tasty. A fresh breeze
was blowing down from the distant mountains, and
the fragrance of jungle flowers filled the air with a
sweet perfume. A bright moon shone in the sky.

"I took your radio out of the Land Rover," Jeff
said, "and set it up. It's just about time for the safari
news—and that's something nobody ought to miss."

He turned a knob, and a young man's voice came
out of the loudspeaker.

"This is KBC, Kenya Broadcasting Company, Nairobi, with the news of the day. The weather tomorrow
will, as usual, be fine. Clear, with no clouds, but with
a light wind from the north. There are reports that
game poachers have been operating in the vicinity of
Thomson's Falls. The commissioner is investigating,
and hunters and guides in that area are requested to
be on the alert." The announcer's voice droned on as
he gave the highlights of the news. "Now," he said at
last, "for messages to parties on safari."

"This is fun," Chuck Warner said to Cherry. "Real
crazy. Listen."

"Message to Mr. Potter on safari with Mr.

Malcolm. Check the setting on your camera carefully, as Keeler's reports that most of your pictures are out of focus. They also caution you not to put your finger in front of the lens."

"Keeler's is the big camera shop in Nairobi," Jeff explained as Cherry giggled.

"Message to Mr. Carter on safari with Mr. Roberts. Your wife has arrived from London and will join your party by midweek.

"Message to Mr. Hayward on safari with Mr. Coe. As per your request for the immediate information, Yale defeated Dartmouth 14 to 6."

Cherry laughed. "This is the funniest radio program I've ever heard."

"Well," Bob said, "it's a link with civilization. And it makes these people, who feel that they are a thousand miles from nowhere, seem close to home."

The messages went on. Then—"Message to Dr. Robert Barton, at Ngogo. Mr. Gikingu has returned to Nairobi this afternoon, a week earlier than expected. He will be in his office whenever it is convenient for you to call."

"Good!" Bob said. "Now we can be getting things going full speed." He flipped the switch of the radio set to "send" and picked up the microphone. "Dr. Barton in Ngogo calling KBC, Nairobi. Dr. Barton in Ngogo calling KBC, Nairobi."

When a voice at the other end of the ether waves answered, Bob said, "Tell Mr. Gikingu that Dr.

Barton will be in his office the day after tomorrow."

"Very well, Dr. Barton," the voice said, and a click ended the connection. "Now," Bob said, "I suggest that we all hit the sack. We've got a big job ahead of us tomorrow."

CHAPTER V

Diamonds Again

CHERRY WAS AWAKENED BY A CHORUS OF BIRDSONG just as the early sun was filtering in through the screening of her little room. She quickly dressed and went outdoors. Tomi, the cook, already had a breakfast fire going on the outdoor grill, and the tantalizing smell of fresh hot coffee hovered pleasantly in the crisp morning air.

Jeff Jordan and Chuck Warner were sitting at the table with steaming mugs in their hands.

"Morning," Jeff said, pouring her a cup of coffee from the big pot bubbling on the grill. "The bacon and eggs are coming right up."

"By tomorrow," Chuck said, "we'll have a shower rigged for you. It won't be fancy, but it will be the best one this side of Nairboi."

Cherry was digging into the big breakfast that Tomi had put before her when Dr. Bob joined the group. "Well," he said as he reached for some coffee, "everybody's up with the chickens!"

"Chuck and I will have the hot water working in two or three hours," Jeff told him.

"Fine! Fine! Then we can start in with our patients, Cherry. Your two helpers are already making sure that the cots have proper bedding. They look like bright, efficient girls."

"Yes, they are," said Cherry. "I found they have good basic, but limited, nursing training. Kavarondi learns a little more quickly than Sara. But Sara has great sympathy and humor—the patients love her already."

By noon Cherry and the two student nurses had all the fifty cots in the clinic made up. They set up a supply closet, a sterilizer, and stocked a first-aid chest. As Jeff had promised, the lighting and water systems were in operation. A stove for heating water and foods was being installed. Still to be completed was a treatment room, where Bob would also have equipment for minor surgery.

Cherry went into the small lab where Bob had laid out his medicines and equipment.

"The hardest part of this job is going to come first," Bob explained, "because once this parasite gets into a victim's blood stream, it usually takes a long time to get rid of it. After we have succeeded in moving all the patients in, making them comfortable and starting their treatments, it will be pretty much routine hospi-

tal procedure from then on. So we'll start by bringing
the worst cases in first. You see to it that each one gets
a good hot bath and is as comfortable as possible. Then
I'll start making blood tests and get ready to administer
the initial medication."

It was hot, tiring work and it went on all afternoon.
Jeff, Chuck, and a pair of their native workmen
carried the patients into the clinic on stretchers that
Tom Gikingu had provided along with the cots.
Under Cherry's supervision, Sara and Kavarondi
bathed each of them in turn in a large canvas tub,
dried them off thoroughly with heavy towels, and
tucked them into bed. Cherry instructed the girls to
sponge-bathe the cases who were in a coma. Cherry
herself prepared treatment trays, and made out charts
to affix beside each patient's cot. Then, as each patient
was put to bed, Bob took a sample of blood which he
sealed carefully in a test tube. Kavarondi wrote each
patient's name—and a number—on a strip of white
adhesive tape which she fastened around his wrist like
a bracelet. Cherry put the number on each tube of
blood for identification.

When the evening shadows had lengthened and
the overhead lights turned on, the drudgery was over.
Thirty-one cases had been processed—twelve women,
ten men, and nine children. Cherry suddenly discovered that she was so tired she could hardly stand on
her feet.

Bob smiled wearily. "Well, that's the lot of them," he said. "Come on and let's have some coffee."

The hot, fragrant coffee put new life into Cherry. She leaned back in the camp chair and breathed a long sigh of relief.

"I don't see how we could have done it," she said at last, "without Sara, Kavarondi, and the boys."

"It would have been a long haul if we'd been working alone, as I was afraid we would have to do in the beginning. There's no getting around it, we've had all the breaks. I'm going to see that Tom Gikingu gets credit for a bang-up job of preparation when I make my first report to the Foundation."

"I'll arrange a night-nursing schedule with the girls," Cherry suggested. "We'll each take an eight-hour duty."

"Suit yourself," Bob said. "But as your doctor I recommend that you let the girls be on duty tonight. You've had a pretty rough few days. My prescription for you is an early dinner, and then early to bed. Then tomorrow you can organize all you like."

Cherry stretched her tired muscles. "Well, I've checked the urgent cases—that infected eye, and the boy with the acute stomach-ache—and they're not so urgent now. On the other cases, Doctor, there is nothing the girls can't handle for a few hours. So I give in."

"Good," Bob said. "Now here are my plans for the next couple of days. After dinner I'm going to run those blood tests, then . . ."

"In that case you'll need some help."

Bob shook his head. "I can do it in no time. I know what I'm going to find, but I want to check just to satisfy myself before I administer any drugs. Then, tomorrow morning, you and I will give our patients their first medication. And after lunch I'll take off for Nairobi to keep my date with Gikingu."

He thought for a moment.

"I had probably better refresh you about this trypanosomiasis bug. As you know, it's a parasite that's introduced into the body by the bite of a tsetse fly. The definite diagnosis is made by finding the parasite in the blood. That's what I'm going to do tonight—even though it's easy enough to recognize the symptoms. The cure is effected by intramuscular injections of Tryparsamide over a period of several weeks. But first, of course, we have to get rid of the flies. That's one thing I'm going to arrange tomorrow."

"A spray plane?"

"Right. I'll see how fast Gikingu can arrange for one. Then we'll do hand spraying too—disinfect every hut in this compound. I'll also get some lime in town and have the workmen whitewash them all inside. I think I brought plenty of drugs with me, but I'll order more sent out from Washington, just to be safe."

"It looks," Cherry said, "as if you'll have a busy day."

"More likely a busy two or three days," Bob said. "Another thing I want to do is arrange for blood specimens to be sent to our labs in Washington. As the cures progress, I'm going to need a more hairline analysis than I am equipped to do in our little lab here. And that goes especially for the samples we'll take from the people who haven't shown any symptoms so far. I can probably arrange to have the test tubes shipped out of Nairobi, on MATS—you know, United States Military Air Transport Service planes, direct to Washington. That will be the fastest and least complicated way."

As they talked, Jeff Jordan strolled up to the fire.

"I've got to hand it to you," he said, shaking his head and smiling. "You've got a real hospital going here."

"We wouldn't have had anything but a load of grief on our shoulders if it hadn't been for what you and Chuck did before we got here," Bob told him. "You're the ones who deserve to take the bows."

Jeff shrugged. "We were just doing a job of work."

"Well," Cherry said, "so were we."

After lunch the next day Bob climbed into his Land Rover, ready to start the long, bumpy ride to Nairobi.

"Our patients looked O.K. this morning when we gave them their shots," he said to Cherry who was leaning against the car with both hands on the door. "But don't expect to see any immediate improvement. Curing this thing is a long pull. Keep an eye on temperatures, but don't worry if you find a little fever now and then. As I told you, it will come and go. Just try to make the patients as comfortable as possible."

"Oh, I forgot to ask you," Cherry said. "Should they have regular morning bed baths?"

"No. As you doubtlessly found out yesterday for yourself, these people aren't used to daily bathing the way Americans are. In this climate, their natural skin-oils are their best protection. And it would do more harm than good to keep them washed away."

He stepped on the starter. "Well, take care. I'll see you in a couple of days."

Cherry thought of something. "I wonder if you could pick up some packages of flower seeds in Nairobi."

"Flower seeds? What kind?"

"Oh, just any kind. The pretty flowers that your mother used to plant in her garden at home. I have an idea."

"Will do," Bob said. "Flower seeds it is."

And the car pulled away trailing a thin cloud of dust.

Cherry had a busy afternoon. She organized her little nursing staff into three eight-hour shifts, so that

Cherry spoon-fed the patients who were seriously ill

either she, Kavarondi, or Sara would be on duty in the clinic around the clock. She arranged for Tomi to keep plenty of antelope stew cooked up, so that her patients could have three light meals a day. Jeff, in turn, arranged for three of his Kikuyu workmen to serve the food, although Cherry or one of the girls had to spoon-feed broth to the cases that were in the worst condition.

About three, Jeff and Chuck went off with the rifle and shotgun they had borrowed from Dr. Bob, and returned to Ngogo just before sundown with two haunches of gazelle and two brace of fat sand grouse. Tomi broiled the grouse for their dinner.

Sitting around the fire after the sun went down, Jeff turned on the radio again to get the news.

Cherry's ears pricked up when she heard the announcer say:

"As a sequel to the attempted diamond smuggling of last week, authorities are investigating rumors of an illegal diamond-mining operation in Northern Rhodesia. We will have more information on this rather startling development as further news is released from Government House."

There it was again! Illicit diamonds! All the questions that had been buzzing through Cherry's head a few days before began to stir around once more.

"What," she asked Jeff, "makes diamond mining unlawful?"

"A lot of things," he replied. "First, diamond

mining is pretty much of a state-controlled monopoly throughout all of Africa. Not only does the government take a whopping big cut, but it regulates the amount of stones that can be sold each year. That's to keep the market price up. Then anywhere you send them—to Europe or the States—the import duty can run up to half the value of the stones. So, you see, if you can locate a secret diamond diggings without notifying the authorities, and then smuggle your stones out of the country without paying any duty, you've got your fortune made overnight."

"And wherever there's the smell of money," Chuck added, "you'll always find enough crooks who try to make it the easy way."

When Cherry fell asleep that night she dreamed about diamonds. Diamond rings—diamond bracelets—whole bushel baskets filled to the brim with the glistening fire-flashing stones.

CHAPTER VI

Kandi

BOB RETURNED TO NGOGO ON THE SECOND EVENING after he had left.

"Well," he said with a tired but happy grin, "everything went fine. That Tom Gikingu is a real go-getter. It took him just one telephone call to arrange for a spray plane. It will be here tomorrow to disinfect the whole area. Then it will make two more trips before the week is out—and that ought to do the job.

"Then I made another phone call, to the MATS commander at Eastleigh Field. A regular cargo plane comes in every day and we can ship out our samples overnight direct to Washington any time we want to. I also brought along half a dozen cases of pressurized spray bombs, and we'll start working on the insides of the huts in the morning."

"Good," Cherry said. "We've already begun on that. Sara and Kavarondi—bless their hearts, they're lifesavers! They have already organized a platoon of women to sweep out all the huts. I put a scarf over my head—just like Mother and I used to do at spring-cleaning time back home—and pitched in with the women. Our two student nurses are with the patients, of course."

"Now don't overdo it, Cherry. You're much more valuable as a nurse than as a cleaning woman."

"Oh, fiddlesticks! A nurse's job is to keep things clean and sanitary. And to teach others how. Besides, it was fun."

"Have it your own way," Bob said. "Now lets take a turn through the wards."

They went first to the men's ward, since Kavarondi—anxious for the doctor's visit—had not yet given the men their supper. On Sara's ward, with fewer and milder cases at this time, women patients were just being served; Cherry checked.

The doctor was pleased at the way Cherry had the hospital running. He stopped beside each patient, to examine him and visit with him briefly, sometimes asking Cherry a question. Bob gave an injection to one man patient, prescribed a medicine for a second, ordered a treatment for a third. Cherry wrote these instructions on the patients' charts. Kavarondi was on duty, and she walked behind them, observing medical procedures and listening to every word—trying her best, Cherry thought, to learn to be a good nurse.

"Kavarondi, you're doing nice work," Dr. Bob said.

The girl glowed at his praise. "You might profitably read an advanced nursing textbook—if Cherry happened to bring one."

"I did, and my two nurses are already studying it." Cherry patted Kavarondi's arm. "I give them surprise quizzes—orals—and they're very good."

When Bob and Cherry reached the end of the row of men's cots, they went on to the women's ward, at the other side of the building. Supper was over, and some of the women patients' children had come to visit them. Bob, Cherry, and Sara—grinning with pride in her patients' good recoveries—made the cot-to-cot tour surrounded by small children. In this ward, as he checked over Sara's patients, Bob decided one woman would need minor surgery and he gave Cherry a few instructions for preparing the woman tomorrow. A skinny, fussy woman who had a harmless rash, and was sure she was terribly sick, was being medicated with bicarbonate tablets and allowed to stay in Sara's care—since Dr. Bob said the woman could do with a rest overnight. Sara managed to keep a straight face about that "medication."

Now Bob and Cherry were through for a few hours, barring emergencies. They went down the steps on the far side of the building; these steps led to Tomi's grill. Bob sniffed the evening breeze.

"That smell of cooking reminds me—I'm hungry enough to eat a horse," he said.

What was cooking was another brace of grouse that

Jeff had bagged that morning. Tomi was roasting them slowly on a spit over the coals. Jeff and Chuck were already at the table, and the four of them ate with the ravenous appetites of healthy young people.

When Tomi had finally cleared the table and replaced the empty plates with tall glasses of iced tea, Bob said to Chuck:

"Would you mind taking the truck into town in the morning and picking up the whitewash lime I ordered? I didn't have room for it in the car."

"I was going in, anyway," Chuck replied. "Jeff and I need some more parts for the electric system."

Cherry suddenly remembered. "Bob, did you get my flower seeds?"

Bob snapped his fingers. "Oh, gosh! I forgot all about them. But Chuck can pick them up for you. And by the way, Cherry, I saw our friend Ed Smith in town. You remember him, the photographer. He said he'd be out here in a few days to start doing his story."

Cherry remembered Ed Smith, all right—and the disturbing impression she'd had of him. But it was too pleasant an evening to puzzle over things that Bob had laughed off as being foolish fancies.

Instead, she said, "Why don't you get your guitar, Chuck, and give us some of those hillbilly songs that you did last night?"

The next week was an exciting and hectic one for Cherry.

Dozens of men, women, and children from nearby villages, who had heard about the new hospital in Ngogo, came in every day for treatment. They had a variety of problems—ranging all the way from broken bones to scratches and skin sores. There were also a few expectant mothers—and of course a few who complained of imaginary ailments as an excuse to see the wonderful "white magic" that the Americans were making. When this word was mentioned, Kavarondi explained that "white magic" was good magic, as opposed to "black magic" which was bad magic. And so, almost from the first day, Cherry and Bob found that they were running a regular day clinic in addition to their primary job of fighting the sleeping sickness epidemic.

Cherry hoped that the government in Nairobi would keep the Ngogo hospital going permanently after the job that she and Bob had come to do was completed.

The spray plane came over on schedule and showered Ngogo, and all the surrounding bush for miles around, with a fine rain of cloudy mist. It was an old-fashioned biplane—an amphibian which could take off and land on water as well as on an airstrip—and was painted a glaring orange color. It made four or five passes over the village, squirting the thin stream of spray from under its lower wing. The spray stung Cherry's eyes and made her cough.

Alarmed, she asked Bob, "Won't this be harmful to the patients?"

"Don't worry about it," he reassured her. "A little bit of this won't hurt a human. But it will get rid of the tsetse flies. That's what's important."

After his last pass, the pilot of the plane zoomed up, waggled his wings as if to say so-long, and disappeared in the direction of Nairobi.

Then they started in on the native huts. All of them had been swept clean, tables, stools, and sleeping pallets. Jeff and Chuck showed their crew of Kikuyu workmen how to work the pressurized spray bombs, and in two days the interiors of all the huts had been thoroughly disinfected. Following that, the workmen did the same for the thatched grass roofs.

Next, the young engineers mixed up huge tubs of lime whitewash, and the crew began to apply the mixture to the inside walls. This job took longer than the spraying, but when it was finished, the interiors were gleaming white and the gloominess of the huts had been replaced by a cheerful brightness. At first the native women had been appalled by what was going on, and a little bit frightened by it all. But when they saw the difference it made in the inward appearance of their homes, they grew cheerful again and even helped the men.

By the end of the first day, all the native workers were covered from head to foot by a thick coat of whitewash. But they washed it off with a mass bath in the river, laughing and splashing around in the water like small, playful boys.

"Isn't it wonderful?" Cherry said to Bob. "They all seem like different people from the ones we saw the first day we were here."

"They are," Bob agreed. "I told you that the chief help these natives needed was learning how to help themselves."

While the men had been spraying and whitewashing the huts, Cherry put her own little private home-improvement project into action. With a hoe she scratched out a small garden plot on either side of the hospital steps. There she planted the flower seeds that Chuck had brought from town. Then she watered the beds and roped the area off with heavy string.

When she was all through, she was not too surprised to see two of the village women standing silently behind her, watching her with puzzled looks on their faces. Each of the women had one or two small children clinging to her long brightly colored skirt.

The younger of the two spoke rapidly to her companion in Swahili, then she said to Cherry in hesitant English, "Is madam sowing mealies?"

Mealies, Cherry knew, was the native corn.

Cherry brushed back a curl of hair that had fallen down over her forehead and gave the women a friendly smile.

"No," she answered, "I am planting flowers." She held up one of the seed packages and pointed to the picture of zinnias on its front. Both women inspected the package closely. "Soon," Cherry went on, "all of this"—she gestured in a sweeping motion over the little garden—"all of this will be a lovely garden of flowers. Won't it be pretty?"

"Pretty!" the younger woman echoed. And the older one, who seemed to speak little or no English, pronounced the word as "Petty!"

The two conversed in Swahili, then the younger one asked timidly, "You help sow flowers for us?"

This was what Cherry had been hoping for. "Certainly," she said. "Which house is yours?"

The woman pointed to the hut nearest the hospital building.

"Me," she said, still smiling.

"Then come on," said Cherry, picking up her hoe and seed packages. "We'll do it right now."

The earth in front of the hut had been trampled down until it was hard, almost solid, underfoot. But Cherry went to work on it with her hoe. The Kikuyu woman stepped around to the back of the hut and reappeared with a crude native hoe of her own. Working side by side, they soon had a small area scratched up on each side of the round, doorless entrance. Cherry then laid out rows, planted the seeds, and roped the plots off with string just as she had done her own.

"Now," Cherry said, standing erect, "in a few weeks you will have a pretty flower garden all your own."

By this time a crowd of perhaps a dozen women had gathered to watch, each one accompanied by two or three small, wide-eyed children. They were talking quietly but animatedly among themselves, gesturing with their hands and shaking their heads.

Now the young woman who had first approached Cherry spoke to them in Swahili. When she had finished, there was a loud hubbub of voices and everyone was smiling from ear to ear.

"They want to know if madam can help them sow flowers too?" the young woman asked Cherry.

Cherry nodded happily. "Tell everybody to get a hoe and you and I will show them how. And tell them I have lots of seeds, enough for everybody."

With much giggling and chattering, the women scattered, each hurrying to her own hut.

Cherry was off duty at the hospital today at these hours, and for the rest of the afternoon she was busy supervising the planting of the gardens. At one point, Bob happened to stroll by. "What's all this?" he wanted to know.

Cherry explained. "The flower beds will make all the difference in the world."

"They sure will," he agreed. "Between whitewashing and landscaping the outsides, we'll have a model town here."

"And a healthy one," Cherry said, "with happy people in it, I hope."

"Maybe the idea will spread all over Kenya," Bob said in a teasing voice. Then he grew serious. "It would certainly be a wonderful thing if it did. You look tired. Why don't you stop now?"

"I was thinking the same thing," Cherry said. "The women know how to do it now. They can get along without me, and I've given them my whole supply of seeds to work with."

After a shower and a change into fresh clothes, Cherry returned to the hospital ward. She was having one last look at her patients when she heard a commotion at the front door. For their day patients, those with minor ailments, and for out-patients, Dr. Bob and Cherry conducted a clinic every morning. The excitement at the door sounded like an emergency. A tall native, wearing khaki shorts and a loose-fitting white T-shirt, came up the steps and into the big room carrying a small boy, about ten years old, in his arms. He was followed by a woman, clearly the boy's mother, who was sobbing softly and reaching out now and then to touch the little fellow's hand or foot. His right foot was an ugly purplish brown and was swollen to nearly twice its normal size.

"Bring him in here," Cherry said, lines of worry creasing her forehead. She led the way between the rows of cots to the little lab in back. "Put him there," she instructed the man, indicating a cot at the side of the room. Then to Sara, who had followed them, she said, "Go quickly and find Dr. Bob."

Sara scampered from the room and Cherry knelt by the bed and looked at the boy. His dark face was slightly gray, and one touch of her fingers to his forehead told her that he was running a high fever. The reason was his swollen, discolored foot.

"Him step on poison stick," the man explained anxiously. "He die?" The boy's mother stood a few feet in the background, her body swaying slightly, her heavy lips trembling.

"No, we won't let him die," Cherry promised. She saw that Kavarondi had entered the room. "What does he mean by poison stick?" she asked.

"He mean scorpion, Miss Cherry," Kavarondi replied. "Very poison. Very bad."

At that moment Bob came in. "What's happened?"

"It seems," Cherry told him, "that the child was stung by a scorpion."

"Let's see," Bob said, and gently picked up the boy's foot to examine it. Then he ordered Kavarondi: "Get all these people out of here."

When they were alone, Bob explained, "This probably happened yesterday, and in the meanwhile the poison has taken hold." He ran his fingers lightly over the instep. "And the stinger broke off; it's still in there." His manner was crisp and workmanlike. "Cleanse the foot with alcohol. First we'll give him an antivenin shot. Then I'll remove the stinger."

This was the first poison-bite case that Cherry had seen in a long time. Anxiety was in her voice as she asked, "Is this—bad?"

"If you mean fatal," Bob replied, "a scorpion sting usually isn't, although it can make you mighty sick. But we got to this young fellow in time. We'll have him up and around in a day or so."

When Cherry had cleansed the foot, Bob injected the antivenin serum in a vein in the boy's calf. Then he made an incision with his lancet and extracted the sharp, curved stinger which was almost half an inch long. Black blood oozed from the wound, and the semiconscious boy groaned as Bob squeezed the sides of the cut to keep the blood coming. Cherry kept wiping it off with cotton-wool soaked in antiseptic.

"That does it," Bob said at last, straightening up. "Bandage him fairly loosely. Then we'll give him something to make him sleep, and put him on a cot out in the ward."

When the treatment was finished, Kavarondi picked the little boy up in her strong arms, carried him out, put him to bed, and covered him with a sheet and blanket.

"Keep an eye on him," Bob said to Cherry. "His temperature should go down in a hurry; but let me know if he doesn't respond the way he should. In the morning I'll take a blood sample to make sure he hasn't been bitten by a tsetse fly as well as a scorpion."

When Cherry made her rounds early the next

morning, she found the little Kikuyu boy sitting up in bed, happily eating a bowlful of hot milk and toast. His face had regained its normal color and his eyes were clear once more.

After Kavarondi had taken away the empty bowl, Cherry removed the bandage from the boy's foot. She saw that the swelling had gone halfway down and the angry red skin around the incision Bob had made was nearly normal again.

The boy certainly has a healthy body, she thought. It was repairing itself the way a good body is meant to.

As she cleansed the foot, preparatory to winding on a new bandage, the boy said, grinning, "Sank you berry much, Missy Sherry. Kavarondi tell me your name."

Cherry was startled that he spoke English so well. Then she remembered Kavarondi telling her that the Kikuyu children picked up English much more readily than most of their parents.

"Now you just hold still," Cherry said, smiling.

"My name Kandi," the boy volunteered.

"Well," Cherry told him, "that's a nice name. Shall I call you Candy? . . . No, I think Sugar Candy would be better."

"I help you," Kandi said eagerly. "I be your houseboy."

"You're going to stay right here in this bed until I tell you to get up," Cherry told him sternly, although she couldn't deny to herself that she was pleased and flattered. Kandi was a charmer, she thought.

"Hi, Kandi! How are you today?" Bob walked up to the bed. He looked Kandi over—grin, foot, and all.

"Well, our patient seems to be greatly improved," the young doctor said to Cherry.

"Yes, his foot is healing nicely," Cherry answered. "I think we may have a little trouble keeping him in bed."

"Keep him there if you have to tie him down." Bob winked at Kandi. "Now we'll take that blood sample." He opened his kit and took out a large syringe.

"This will sting a little," Cherry told Kandi as she swabbed the inside of his forearm with alcohol. "But you're a brave boy, Kandi. Don't look at your arm, look over your shoulder."

"Kandi do what you say, Missy Sherry."

He couldn't help wincing as Bob plunged the needle into a vein and drew out a sample of blood. But the white-toothed grin never left his face.

Cherry patted him on the cheek. "Now you keep on being a good boy, Kandi, and do what Kavarondi and Sara tell you. Maybe we can let you out of bed by tomorrow."

"Then I be your houseboy, Missy Sherry?"

"O.K.," Cherry said. "Then we'll see about you being my houseboy."

"You seem to have made a conquest," Bob remarked as they went toward the lab.

"Well, I couldn't have made a nicer one," Cherry said. "Isn't he simply the cutest thing you ever saw?"

Bob put a drop or two of Kandi's blood under the lens of his microscope and examined it closely.

"Looks perfectly normal," he finally said. "But I'll send it along to Washington just to make doubly sure. And that reminds me. After we've had some breakfast, you and I will get to work taking specimens from all the people here in the village who don't seem to have been infected."

Over hot cakes and coffee in front of Tomi's grill, Cherry heard the roar of a plane in the sky. Looking up, she saw the spray plane flying low over the hills, spilling out its familiar streamer of cloudy mist.

"Thank goodness," she said, "this is the third and last time. That thing bothers me."

"It bothers the tsetse flies a whole lot more," Bob declared. "By now all of them ought to be cleared out of this entire valley." Then he added, "Everything is coming along fine, Cherry—'way ahead of the schedule I had set up in my mind originally. As a matter of fact, if things keep going as well as they have up until now, our worst troubles are over."

As Cherry, Bob, Jeff, and Chuck watched, the amphibian—instead of zooming up and heading back for Nairobi—touched down on the water of the river.

The pilot throttled down his engine and taxied up onto the sandy bank on the wheels that he had let down on either side of the float. The side door opened and a familiar figure stepped out. Over his shoulder he had a canvas duffel bag, and two cameras hung by straps around his neck. A big smile wreathed his face.

It was Ed Smith, the photographer.

"Hi, folks!" he said cheerfully. "It looks as if I made it just in time for breakfast!"

CHAPTER VII

The Orange Airplane

"MAKE YOURSELF AT HOME, SMITH," BOB SAID AS he walked over to the plane. "And you too," he said to the pilot. "You could use a bite, couldn't you?"

"Don't mind if I do," the pilot replied. Smith introduced him as Gus Fisher. He was a tall, thin scarecrow of a man; his khaki slacks and a cotton windbreaker hung on him. "At least I can use a minute or two to stretch. That cockpit is small for me."

In a few moments the visitors were digging into heaping plates of Tomi's hot cakes and washing them down with steaming mugs of coffee.

"I had intended to rent a Land Rover for the trip," Ed Smith said at last. "But I happened to be at the airport yesterday and learned that Gus Fisher here was flying in today to spray the place. So I bummed a ride." He and the pilot exchanged a glance; something understood and special. Cherry noticed that glance, and wondered. Smith spread his hands in an expansive gesture. "And here I am, all set to do the story of the year."

"Ed is going to make us all famous," Bob said to Chuck and Jeff. And he explained the photographer's mission. "I've told him he can have free run of the place. So if you see him snooping around with those cameras of his, think nothing of it."

Smith chuckled. "Snooping is a rather unkind word, Doctor. Any magazine photographer usually has to expose several dozen rolls of film in order to get ten or twelve of the right kind of pictures for a story. So I actually will be aiming my lenses at just about everything in sight." He looked around. "You certainly have made a lot more progress here than I would have imagined you could in such a short time."

Bob told him about the preliminary work the young engineers had done. The photographer asked them a few questions. Bob, meanwhile, briefed Cherry on their day's work in the clinic.

Cherry expected her patients would ask her who came in the orange plane. She herself was fascinated by the color of the plane. Up close, the dazzling orange paint, almost luminescent in its glowing intensity, reacted on her eyes like the rays of a bright light suddenly flashed into them.

"That's a mighty fancy plane you have there, Mr. Fisher," she said, teasing the pilot. "It looks like Times Square in New York all lighted up at night."

"Now don't you go making remarks about my taste in colors, Miss Ames," the pilot replied with a smile in his voice. "That paint is purely for self-protection."

"Protection?"

"That's right. You see, I'm what you call a free-lance bush pilot. I fly charter trips all over this rough country here in Kenya, and often over the rain forests of southern Tanganyika and the Rhodesias. Now if something went wrong, and I had to make a forced landing, I would radio for a rescue plane. But if my ship was painted gray or green, a search plane could fly a hundred feet straight over my head and never see me. On the other hand, this bright orange stands out, as you say, like Forty-second Street and Broadway. A pilot looking for me could spot me ten miles away."

Cherry laughed. "I'm sorry. I just never saw a plane the color of yours."

"It's my own invention, Miss Ames. I don't know why other bush pilots don't paint their planes the same way. Maybe they're superstitious; maybe they think it's asking for an accident. But you can just call me Safety-First Gus."

After a little while the pilot said, "Well, I've got to hop off. If a couple of you fellows will help me get my plane turned around, I'll take her back to town."

Jeff and Chuck jumped to their feet to lend a hand, and soon they had the amphibian pointed toward the water. Gus, bent nearly double, squeezed into the cockpit. He started the engine, and in a minute or two was taxiing up the narrow river. Then the engine roared louder, the ship put on a burst of speed, lifted off the surface, and rose gracefully over the treetops.

Smith got to his feet. "Well," he said, "with your permission, I'll look around the place, before I try to take any pictures. O.K. if I leave my cameras here for a while?"

"Help yourself," Bob told him. "And if there's anything you want, just ask for it."

"We have an extra tent," Jeff said. "Chuck and I will fix it up for you and put in a cot and a table."

"That's swell, fellows." Ed Smith smiled brightly at them all, with a special gleam at Cherry. She did not respond. The photographer's smile remained fixed and very bright. "Just swell of all of you. But I don't want to put you to any extra trouble."

"No trouble at all," Jeff said. "Just be sure you get some good pictures of us so I can send one home to my girl."

After breakfast everybody went to work. Chuck and Jeff were installing permanent electrical and plumbing fixtures to replace the temporary ones they had put in so that the hospital would be workable at once. Ed Smith was looking over every nook and cranny of the village to get ideas for his pictures. Cherry and Bob were taking blood samples from the people in Ngogo who had shown no symptoms of the sleeping sickness. Kavarondi had rounded up some of these persons—about a dozen of them stood in line outside the laboratory door—and was ushering them in one at a time.

As each blood sample was taken, Kavarondi put a bracelet of adhesive tape around the person's wrist and wrote his name and number on it. Bob then put the same number on the test tube of blood—the same procedure they had used with the people who were hospitalized. Cherry, Bob, and Kavarondi kept on taking blood samples until midafternoon.

At last Bob said, "I guess that's as much as we can do this afternoon. Please clean the equipment, Kavarondi, and put it away. Cherry, where are those record forms?" The young doctor wiped his forehead. "I'll run my preliminary tests later this evening, and we'll have the whole thing done in a day or two. Whew! Me, I'm for a long, cool glass of iced tea, in this heat."

As they were finishing up, Ed Smith came in. "Say, this looks interesting." He bent over the rack of test tubes, peering. "What are all these?"

Bob explained how blood samples were being taken of all the people in the town; how he was running his own tests on them; and, how later, he was going to send them to the Abercrombie laboratory in Washington for a closer analysis.

"Well, I must say, Doc, that you do things pretty thoroughly—even back here in this jungle wilderness."

The doctor did not look flattered. He said:

"With any medical problem, lab analysis is a must. You know that, Smith, especially with a problem as tough as this one."

Smith backed off and began to examine possible camera angles of the little lab through a square that he made with his thumbs and forefingers.

"We'll have some interesting pictures here," he said when he was finished. "I want to get some of you and Miss Ames actually taking the samples—and of course of this young woman here." He nodded at Kavarondi. "Now how do you send these test tubes to the States?"

Bob showed him a small cardboard box, divided inside into twelve narrow compartments. "The tubes," he said, "as you can see, are sealed with these rubber stoppers. Then we'll pack the whole carton tightly with cotton. And I have made arrangements with the Military Air Transport to fly them directly to our people in Washington."

"Good planning," the photographer said.

"Did you find the village interesting?" Bob asked.

"You bet," Smith said. "I explored all of it. I think I'll load my cameras tomorrow morning and get down to work."

After dinner that evening the Americans sat around the table, listening as usual to the KBC newscast.

When the personal messages were over, Bob flipped the switch to "send" and got off a progress report to Tom Gikingu in Nairobi.

"Look," Ed Smith said. "Since that radio of yours is two-way, do you mind if I send a message into town?"

"Help yourself," Bob told him.

Smith picked up the mike. "This is Ed Smith with the Abercrombie medical party at Ngogo. Could you get this message to Mr. Simon at the New Stanley?"

"Go ahead," the voice in Nairobi said.

"Here's the message. Quote. I have my story angle figured out. Contact me here within a few days. End quote."

He put the mike back on its hook. "Simon is the *Click* representative for Africa," he explained. "And by good luck he happens to be in Nairobi this week."

"Well," Cherry said to herself, "I guess I was wrong. He really does know the people at the magazine." And she remembered what Bob had said about her being too suspicious.

CHAPTER VIII

The Pretty Pebble

IT WAS A BEAUTIFUL SUNDAY MORNING. THE SUN burned bright and hot over the grove of acacia trees, and songbirds caroled merrily in the thickets.

The past four days had been ones of intense activity for everyone in Ngogo. Cherry and Bob had finished the first round of blood tests. All the patients in the hospital had been given their second injection of Tryparsamide, and a few were showing definite signs of improvement. "But don't think we have licked the thing overnight," Bob cautioned Cherry. "Trypanosomiasis strikes like a cobra and leaves like a snail, as the saying goes."

Bob had taken his initial batch of blood samples to the airport and seen them safely off to Washington. Ed Smith, saying that he wanted to take some film into town to be developed, had gone with him.

But now it was a quiet Sunday; a day of rest for all hands.

Little Kandi had recovered beautifully from his scorpion sting, and now he had taken to following Cherry around like a faithful puppy dog. At the moment he was sitting on the thin grass at her feet, ready to jump up instantly if she needed anything. He persisted in calling himself "Missy Sherry's houseboy," and as such he had adopted a superior attitude toward the other children in the village.

"I have an idea," Jeff Jordan said. "Let's go on a picnic. You remember that little pool we found up on the bend in the river, Chuck? It would be a perfect spot."

"Wonderful!" Cherry beamed. "I haven't been on a picnic since I don't know when." She jumped up. "Come on, Kandi. Let's go help Tomi fix some food."

"Not me, pal," Chuck said. "I'm not gonna move out of this shade. You all have fun."

"Count me out, too," Ed Smith added. "This sun is just right for color pictures—and I don't want to let it go to waste."

"Well, how about you, Doctor?" Jeff asked.

"No," Bob replied. "I have things to do. But why don't you take Kavarondi? She's been working hard, and I'm sure she'd enjoy the outing."

Half an hour later, Cherry, Kavarondi, and Jeff rounded a bend in the river and approached the quiet pool. Jeff carried the lunch basket. Kandi tagged along, stopping now and then to pick wildflowers. Suddenly Jeff grabbed Cherry's arm and pulled her to a halt. "Sh-h!" he whispered. "Don't make a sound! Just look at that!"

A small, tan antelope that had been swimming in the river sank down out of sight at the sound of their approach. Presently he emerged, with only his eyes, his ears, and his nostrils protruding above the water. Then he disappeared again, and they saw no more of him.

"My gracious!" Cherry gasped. "Did the poor thing drown?"

"No, he's O.K.," Jeff said. "That was a sitatunga. He's the only antelope in the world that can swim under water. When he senses danger, he just submerges like a submarine, and away he goes. They are so rare that the natives say it's good luck to see them. I've heard about them, but I never figured I'd ever actually run into one."

They walked on to the small beach that rimmed the pool. Papyrus-like reeds grew at the water's edge, and huge purple flowers blossomed from thick vines that climbed up the trees. Great butterflies, three or four times as large as any that Cherry had ever seen, hovered in the sweet-scented air.

Jeff spread out a blanket and put the lunch basket down upon it. Kandi had wandered down to the water and began to play along the bank. Kavarondi sat in the shade of a tree, reading the nursing manual

Cherry had loaned her. Cherry and Jeff leaned back and let the bright sun shine into their faces.

"What's your girl like?" Cherry asked.

"My girl?"

"The one back in the States."

"Where did you get the idea that I had a girl back in the States?" Jeff wrinkled his brows.

"The other day you asked Mr. Smith to be sure and take a good picture of you so you could send it home to your girl."

Jeff laughed. "Oh, I was just saying that for fun. But now if I *did* have a girl back home, she'd be—let's see"—he studied Cherry's face with mock serious-ness—"she'd have coal-black hair, and dark eyes— And, oh yes, she'd be a nurse so that she could take good care of me if I caught a cold or broke an arm or something."

"Well," Cherry interrupted, smiling, "ask a silly question and you get a silly answer."

"I don't know what is so silly about that," Jeff said. "I was just describing my idea of a pretty girl."

As Jeff spoke, Kandi ran up from the water's edge calling excitedly. "Missy Sherry! Missy Sherry! Look at the pretty pebble Kandi find!"

In his hand he held a white, oval-shaped stone, about the size of a bird's egg, which he dropped proudly into Cherry's palm. The stone sparkled and glistened in the sun, reflecting rays of the bright sunlight from its smoothly polished surface. The

"Missy Sherry! Look at the pretty pebble Kandi find!"

thought of diamonds flashed through Cherry's mind as she turned the stone round and round and looked at it closely.

"Jeff," she said, "you remember the news story we heard on the radio the other night—about the diamond strike somewhere around here? Do you think that this could possibly be a rough diamond?"

Jeff examined the pretty pebble. "I wish it was," he said at last. "I'm no mineralogist, but I know enough about stones to know that this is just a nice piece of quartz crystal, worth about a dollar as a rock collector's item. It's been rolling around on the bottom of this river for maybe a thousand years or more—scraping against sand and other rocks—and that's how it got its high polish." He shook his head and grinned. "Africa is full of diamonds—that's for sure. But this isn't one of them. And besides, you don't find diamonds north of Tanganyika."

Cherry gave the stone back to Kandi. "Keep it for your little sister," she said. "Now let's dig into that lunch basket. I'm hungry."

They got back to the hospital just as the fiery sun was setting over the western mountains. Bob, Chuck, and Ed Smith were lounging in canvas chairs in front of the outdoor fire. Bob was reading a medical journal, but put it aside.

"We were lucky," Cherry told them. "We saw a sitatunga."

"A what?"

Jeff explained about the diving antelope.

"And Kandi found a diamond," Cherry went on.

Ed Smith jumped up from his chair. "You found a *diamond?* What do you mean a diamond?" His eyes popped with excitement.

"Oh, you needn't get so excited, it wasn't a real diamond," Cherry said. "Although it looks like one. It's just a pretty piece of—what did you say, Jeff?—quartz. Show the gentleman, Kandi."

The photographer settled back into his chair with a sigh of relief. Cherry wondered whether Smith was always so excitable. Or only on certain subjects, like diamonds?

"You know," Bob said reflectively, "that was how the first African diamond was found—by a boy playing along a riverbank. And it was that diamond that caused the rush of European settlers, and built Africa up to the great country it is becoming now."

"Maybe Africa would be better off today," Jeff said, "if the boy had thrown the diamond back into the water and white men had never come here at all."

Bob shrugged. "Who knows? Speaking of white man's civilization, how would you like to drive Cherry into Nairobi tomorrow? There are a few things I need, and she hasn't been out of camp since we first got here. Cherry, can Kavarondi and Sara manage the clinic without you for a few hours?"

Cherry thought. "Yes, if I have two hours first to set up the day's work. And I must give three treatments.

And if no emergencies! Mondays can be busy. With all those *ifs*—hmm— Yes, can do." She smiled. "A girl likes to go shopping now and then, even if she really doesn't need anything."

Nairobi's streets were bustling with traffic as always when Jeff drove the Land Rover up in front of the New Stanley Hotel and parked.

"Go get the shopping out of your system," Jeff told her, "and I'll meet you back here in an hour or so."

Walking along the broad sidewalk, Cherry felt like a Kenya veteran. Her face was browned from exposure to the broiling bush-country sun, her khaki clothes had been laundered just often enough not to look brand new like a greenhorn's, and her hair—That's what she'd do! She'd stop in at the first beauty shop she saw!

Two hours later, as she sat on the wide hotel veranda reflecting that nothing perked up a girl quite so much as having her hair done, Jeff came bounding up the steps. His face was flushed and his voice rang with excitement.

"Come on and see the fun! There's a lion loose at the airport."

"You're joking!" Cherry gasped. "A real, live wild lion?"

"That's what a fellow down the street said. Hop in the car and we'll go see for ourselves."

At Eastleigh Airport a cordon of police was holding

back the small crowd that had gathered. A dozen men, some of them with guns, had lassoed the lion and were tugging and pulling to get it into a large iron-barred cage. The animal was a small male, Cherry saw, with just the beginnings of a black mane, and he was putting up a stubborn, if losing, battle for his freedom.

"It seems the little beggar wandered in from the parkland last night," a tall man with an English accent replied to Jeff's question. "And he frightened a group of tourists half out of their wits this morning just as they were disembarking from a BOAC plane."

Cherry smiled to herself, thinking that a lion rampaging around the airport was a good introduction to Africa for tourists. "They'll be telling the story to their grandchildren," she said to Jeff.

"Yes," Jeff replied, "and when we tell Smith about this, he'll be mighty sorry he didn't come with us. Boy! What a picture this would make for his magazine story!"

At last the game wardens managed to haul the young lion into the cage, lock it, and get it onto a truck. "Well, I guess the show is over," Jeff said. "They'll take the youngster back out to the park—and I'll bet he will never wander off the reservation again."

As they turned to walk back to their car, Cherry saw a bright orange plane sitting beside a hangar. With that color, it could only be the plane that Gus

Fisher had flown into their camp. And, sure enough, she recognized the tall, skinny pilot, leaning against the lower wing, talking to a slightly built man. The pilot reached into the cockpit and brought out a small briefcase which he handed to his companion. When the man reached for it, he turned halfway around and Cherry saw his face. With a start, she recognized the little Greek trader they had seen in the Cairo café. What was his name? Suddenly she remembered—Krynos! That was it. She waved a greeting to them. The motion of her arm caught their eyes. Both men looked up, and when they saw her, quickly turned their faces away without any sign of recognition. Krynos strode off and climbed into a waiting car. The scarecrow pilot squeezed into the orange plane.

What a strange way to act, Cherry thought. She was sure they must have seen her. She tried to tell herself that it didn't matter. But for both of them to avoid her—it was odd.

"That pilot sure was right," Jeff said, cutting into her thoughts. "You can spot his plane a mile away. But he didn't recognize us when you waved."

CHAPTER IX

Visitors

~~~~~~

WALKING THROUGH THE COMPOUND AFTER LUNCH the next day, Cherry was encouraged by all the changes she and the others had helped to make in the little village of Ngogo. The inner walls of the native huts gleamed with their coats of whitewash. The flower seeds that had been planted in the dooryards had already begun to sprout, thanks to the hot African sun and the rich, black African soil.

The hospital and the day clinic were busier than ever. But Kavarondi and Sara had proved to be apt pupils, and they had taken much of the routine work off Cherry's shoulders, making daily progress reports on every patient. One of Cherry's chief responsibilities—and one that she didn't feel she could yet pass along to the student nurses—was helping Dr. Bob take regular blood samples from each sleeping-sickness patient for analysis.

Sometimes, in the evenings, she gathered groups of

the children around her on the hospital steps, or in front of Tomi's fire, and told them stories—Aesop's fables, Mother Goose, and tales from American folklore like Johnny Appleseed, Paul Bunyan, and Davy Crockett. Often the older people of the village would come up quietly and sit around the edges of the group. And now and then one of them would respond in kind by retelling the age-old legends of Africa. Since the tribes of this part of Africa had no written language, such tales as these were their only way of handing down past history from generation to generation. And from them, Cherry thought, she learned more about the real Africa, in terms of its people and its customs, than in any of the books she had read.

Today, as she rounded the clinic building, she heard the roar of a motor and the screech of tires. When she got to the front steps, she saw Bob and Jeff standing beside the jeep that had just pulled up.

"Look who's here, Cherry," Bob shouted. "It's our old friend from Cairo."

Sure enough, the man behind the wheel was Spiro Krynos.

"Good afternoon, Miss Ames," the Greek said with his slight accent. "It is most pleasant to see you once again." He stepped out of the car and offered his hand.

"We almost met yesterday afternoon," Cherry said. "Out at the Nairobi airport when the men were chasing that lion."

Krynos shook his head, a puzzled look on his face.

"No-o," he said slowly, "it couldn't have been me. I've spent the last two days up north and haven't been in Nairobi for a week." He smiled his friendly smile. "You must have seen someone who looked like me. Although I wouldn't wish that resemblance on anyone."

Cherry knew that the man was lying, but she couldn't imagine why. Well, she reasoned, it was his business—although it troubled her. What had he received from Gus Fisher, in that briefcase?

"What brings you out this way, Mr. Krynos?" Bob asked.

"You may recall," Krynos replied, "that I told you I was a dealer in pyrethrum. I came down here to look over the new crop. When I remembered that you were going to establish your hospital here, I thought to stop by and say hello."

Ed Smith came up to the group and was introduced to the newcomer.

"Now that you're here," Bob said, "you may as well stay for dinner and spend the night. It might interest you to see what we've done."

Krynos bowed and protested he did not want to put them to any trouble.

"There's plenty of room in my tent," Smith suggested, "if you can locate another cot, Jeff." Jeff nodded.

"In that case," Krynos said, "I accept with pleasure." He looked around at the hospital building and the spruced-up huts. "It isn't often that you see a village like this back here in the jungle. You people have worked miracles; and I will admit that I'd like to look around."

"Feel free to wander around the place all you please," Bob said.

"I'll lead the guided tour," Smith offered, "since all you people probably have work to do."

Bob, Cherry, and Jeff went off to attend to their various duties. Krynos took his duffel bag from the jeep and carried it into Smith's tent. Then the two of them set out on an inspection tour of the installation.

Night comes down fast on the equator, with hardly any twilight at all. It almost seems as though it is full daylight one minute and complete darkness the next. And the last light of the sun had just disappeared over the distant mountains when another car came roaring up the trail and into camp.

"This certainly is our day for company," Bob remarked, peering through the gloom at the approaching headlights. Then a small truck rolled into the light that bathed the eating area, and stopped. This time it was the white hunter, Long Jack Robertson, who stepped out of the cab.

"Hello, folks," he greeted them, a big grin on his face. His khaki clothes were stained with dust and sweat; and the double brim of his wide safari hat

"Hello, folks!" Long Jack greeted them

sagged down just the way a professional hunter's should, Cherry thought.

"I brought you some fresh meat for the pot." Jack snapped a few words in Swahili to Tomi, who was stirring the coals in his grill getting ready to cook dinner. Broad-shouldered, muscular Tomi hurried around to the back of the truck and lifted out an antelope.

"Your boy will know what to do with it," Jack said. He dropped his long body into a canvas chair.

"Jack, you're a sight for sore eyes," Bob told him. Then he introduced him to Jeff, Chuck, and Krynos. "I believe you've already met Ed Smith here."

"No, can't say that I have," the hunter replied as they shook hands.

"Hmm!" Cherry said to herself. "What about that evening in the New Stanley?" But she didn't voice her thought out loud. Here were two deliberate lies in the same afternoon. She *had* seen Krynos at the airport, and Smith talking with Long Jack in the hotel lobby. Krynos looked like the sort of man who might want to hide something. But not the white hunter, Cherry thought. The white hunter appeared straightforward. She was puzzled.

Long Jack was talking. "I've got a party in camp just about two miles from here, so I thought I'd run over and see how you were making out."

"Gun hunters or camera hunters, Jack?" Bob asked.

"Camera hunters this time. Americans. A man and his wife. And pretty wealthy Americans too, judging by all the luxuries we brought along—bathtubs, a portable electric system, a refrigerator, and whole cases of fancy canned food."

"It looks as if you're having a vacation instead of a safari," Bob suggested.

"Not so you can notice it," the hunter said. "I've taken more risks with this camera chap—Porter is his name—than with most of the trophy hunters I've guided." He thought for a moment. "Just the other day, for example, over on the Serengeti Plain. You remember it, Bob. We hunted there with your dad."

Bob nodded.

"Well, Porter had said that he wanted a motion picture of a charging rhino. So that afternoon, cruising around in the Land Rover, we found one grazing all by himself. He was a big one, too, and he looked mean. We drove up to within a hundred yards or so of him, and my client set up his tripod. The old rhino got wind of us, and started swaying his shoulders and pawing up the ground. I stood just behind and a little to the left of Porter with my big double-barrel .460 rifle ready to shoot if I had to. My client began to grind his camera, and then the old boy charged straight for us."

Cherry was listening, wide-eyed, to the hunter's story.

"Then Porter spoke up, calm as if he did this every

day," Long John went on. " 'Remember not to shoot
until I say so' he said. 'I want him to get as close as
possible.'

"The beast was coming at us like an express train,
with that hooked horn low and his little pig eyes
squinting, and his weight making the ground shake.
When he was about thirty feet away, I thought Porter
had either forgotten about giving me a signal, or was
too scared to speak. And I was just squeezing my hand
on the trigger, when the old rhino skidded to a stop,
looked at us for a minute in a sort of puzzled way, and
then trotted off to one side as though he thought the
whole thing was pretty silly."

Cherry whistled. "My goodness! Do you mean he
stopped charging, just like that?"

"Rhinos are odd beasts, Miss Ames," Jack explained. "They do unpredictable things, and nobody
knows what goes on in those strange little brains of
theirs. Anyway, Porter was tickled to death about
getting such a good picture. But I don't mind saying
the whole thing gave me quite a turn. I didn't dare try
to help my client with his camera equipment lest he
see how badly my hands were shaking."

While everyone laughed at Jack's story, the hunter
was looking intently at Ed Smith.

"You know, Mr. Smith," he said at last, "I believe
you and I *did* meet briefly in Nairobi a week or so ago.
You're a photographer too, aren't you? And didn't you

ask me something about getting some safari pictures for a magazine?"

Smith looked sheepish. "Yes," he said, "we did meet. But since you seemed to have forgotten, I didn't want to embarrass you."

"Sorry, Mr. Smith." The hunter smiled apologetically.

Cherry felt a little ashamed of her earlier suspicion of Long Jack and Smith.

"Actually," Smith went on, "I'd like to talk some more about a safari sometime. For instance, would I have to buy a hunting license if I wanted you to back me up with a gun the way you did Porter?"

"That all depends," the hunter began.

Bob got to his feet. "I've got a few things to do before dinner," he said.

"And I'd better look at Kavarondi's evening report," Cherry said.

Jeff and Chuck also remembered last-minute chores, and soon the hunter was left explaining licenses and other safari details to Smith, as Spiro Krynos puffed on a long cigar.

Listening to the radio news after dinner had become a sort of nightly ritual, and Cherry never ceased to be amused at the messages. When they were over, Long Jack took his leave, saying that he wanted to see his clients safely bedded down for the night.

Then Bob flipped the radio switch to "send."

When he got the operator in Nairobi, he said, "This is Dr. Barton in Ngogo. Will you please get a message to Major Welsh at the United States Military Air Transport office that I will have another shipment to go to the Abercrombie Institute in Washington, D. C., on tomorrow's plane?"

The voice on the other end repeated the message and then clicked off.

"I wish," Bob said, when he had hung the mike back on its hook, "that I didn't have to take tomorrow off to go into Nairobi. I wanted us to begin the next series of Tryparsamide injections, Cherry. But those blood samples have to get off on schedule."

"I guess Jeff or I could go," Chuck suggested.

Ed Smith spoke up. "I was going to go to town the next time one of you did. I'd like to see how that latest batch of film I left at Keeler's turned out. So I'll drive your car in and leave your package at the field."

"Good," Bob said. "Just deliver it to Major Welsh at Eastleigh, but be sure you get it there before three o'clock."

The next morning, as soon as breakfast was over, Mr. Krynos said to Bob:

"Thank you so much for your hospitality, Doctor. But I think I had better be off. I want to drive over to Nisi, on Lake Victoria, and I feel I should get an early start."

"You're welcome any time," Bob replied, pleased.

"I can't tell you how much I have enjoyed my visit

with you. It has been a most happy coincidence."

"A coincidence?" Bob asked. "I don't quite . . ."

Krynos smiled. "Oh, I mean meeting the white hunter with the curious name—what was it, Long Jack?—and hearing his adventurous stories. And also Mr. Smith, here, who has told me about the pictures he is taking."

"I'll go get your bag," Smith volunteered. "I'm taking off, too, in a little while, but I'm going the other way."

Ed Smith went into his tent and came out in a moment with the trader's duffel bag.

"There you are," he said, putting the bag into the back of Krynos' car. He stuck out his hand. "Nice to have met you."

Krynos said good-bye all around, and in a few minutes his jeep had disappeared through the trees down the trail.

About an hour later the photographer walked into the lab where Bob and Cherry were putting the tubes of blood specimens into a cardboard box and carefully packing them in cotton. He had a small canvas airlines bag in his hand. Cherry wondered if the bag held films.

"Well, I'm all set to go," Smith said.

Bob wrapped the box in heavy brown paper, tied it securely, and addressed it. Then he repeated his instructions as to how Smith was to find Major Welsh at the MATS office.

"Don't worry," Smith assured him. "I'll see that it gets there safe and sound."

He carried the package out to Bob's Land Rover, put the package and his bag on the seat beside him, and roared out of camp.

It was almost sundown when Ed Smith returned. "I got your carton to the MATS people on time," he said, "and then spent most of the rest of the afternoon at Keeler's. You'll be happy to know that my pictures turned out swell. I airmailed them to the office in New York."

As he was talking, Cherry's sharp eyes spotted a dark reddish-brown stain on the sleeve of his bush jacket.

"What happened?" she asked curiously, pointing to the blotch. "It looks like blood. Did you cut yourself?"

Smith looked at the stain, and for a moment seemed at a loss for words. "Why—I—no—" he stammered. "I didn't cut myself." Then he smiled. "We were fooling around with developing chemicals in Keeler's darkroom and I guess some splashed on my arm. And the heck of it is," he said wryly, "it probably won't wash out."

That was odd, Cherry thought. Her brother Charlie was a camera bug, and had his own darkroom back home in Hilton. But she had never seen any developing chemical that was a dark red!

~~~~~~

CHAPTER X

The Yellow Stone

BUT CHERRY'S CURIOSITY ABOUT ED SMITH FADED as nothing unusual happened. The days at the jungle hospital sped swiftly by. They were happy days for Cherry, filled with the sights and the sounds and the wonderfully clear sunshine of tropical Africa.

"Why do people persist in calling this Darkest Africa?" she asked Jeff late one afternoon after work, as they were strolling along the river. "I will always think of it as Brightest Africa."

The days were filled, too, with a rewarding sense of accomplishment. All of the trypanosomiasis cases were responding to the treatment that she and Dr. Bob administered. Most of the patients that had been brought into the ward in a coma had come around nicely. Many of them were allowed out of bed to walk about in the sunlight of the compound for a little while each day. Best of all, only three new cases had developed—and they proved to be light ones that Bob's medication had caught in time.

Chuck Warner had gone back to Nairobi two days ago to go to work on another Abercrombie assignment. But Jeff stayed on as a permanent member of the Ngogo staff. Ed Smith had also continued to hang around, snapping his cameras incessantly. "This will be the greatest African story *Click* has ever published," he said to Cherry one evening. "And you are going to have a starring role in it."

"I can do without your flattery," Cherry thought. She still did not like Smith. Yet maybe, after all, she had jumped to some hasty conclusions about him, Cherry told herself. He did seem like a pleasant, friendly man, at least on the surface.

Then one morning Long Jack Robertson drove into the village in his safari truck. Again he brought a good-sized antelope which he said was "meat for the pot."

"I took my people over to the Ngorongoro Crater for a couple of days," he said at lunch. "And Mr. Porter had the time of his life. He practically worked his cameras to death."

"I don't wonder," Bob said. "I remember Ngorongoro as the most fabulous place in Africa—or most likely in all the world."

"What an odd name," Cherry remarked. "And what makes it so fabulous?"

The white hunter looked thoughtful. "Ngorongoro is the crater of a long-dead volcano. Its walls are a thousand feet straight down, and at the bottom is a lush, level meadow that is about fifteen miles across. You get down to it from the rim by a narrow winding trail. And once you're there, it's like a paradise. The herds of animals have been completely cut off from the rest of the world for centuries, and the animals themselves are perfect specimens. I guess Ngorongoro is what all of Africa must have looked like before the white men and the trophy hunters swarmed in to spoil it."

"If you and I ever do make that camera safari I was talking about," Ed Smith said, "that's the first place I want to go."

"Look here," Long Jack said, snapping his fingers, "that gives me an idea. I only have three more days with the Porters until I take them back to Nairobi. And I had planned to safari down through the bush country west of here to give Porter one last crack at elephants. Why don't you come along? I'm certain my client would welcome some advice from a professional photographer."

Smith looked eager. "You're sure it would be all right with your people?"

"Sure I'm sure. The Porters are nice. You'd be somebody new to talk to. And, as I said, you could give him some valuable tips."

Ed Smith look pleased. "In that case, I can't resist. It will give me some atmosphere shots to round out my story. I'll pack a duffel bag and be with you in half a minute."

"When are you and I going to make another safari, Bob?" the hunter asked. "Bathtubs and electric lights and refrigerators are O.K. But every now and then I like to get out on a shooting trip and rough it with a chap like yourself who likes to hunt the hard way."

"Not right away, I'm afraid," Bob replied. "But I promised Miss Ames a camera safari after our work here is cleaned up."

"That's fine, Bob. You know where to reach me."

Smith came out of his tent laden with his camera and his bag.

"Let's go," the hunter said. Then to Bob: "I'll drop Smith off in a couple of days on our way back to town."

He stepped on the starter and the truck rolled down the trail and out of sight.

As usual, Kandi was underfoot that afternoon, pestering Cherry about chores that he could do for her.

Cherry patted the top of his curly head. "Well now," she said, "one thing you can do that would help us a lot would be to go over and straighten up Mr. Smith's tent. See that everything is tidied up and the bed is made. Mr. Smith will like that when he gets back from his trip."

The boy eagerly ran off. She forgot all about him

until, an hour later, he came rushing up to her as she was leaving the clinic after her regular inspection tour.

"Look, Missy Sherry," he said. "Kandi find another pretty pebble."

Cupped in his outstretched palm was a large canary-yellow stone that gleamed in the afternoon sun. She took it from him and inspected it closely. It was smaller than the piece of quartz the boy had picked up at the river, but it had a more lustrous sheen. There seemed to be highlights in it that caught the sun's rays and threw them back into her eyes.

"Did you get this down by the river where you found the other one?" she asked curiously.

"No, missy. Kandi find it under Mista Smith's cot in his tent."

Cherry was stunned. Disconnected incidents flashed through her mind—the news of finding rough diamonds—Ed Smith's excitement when Kandi thought he had found a diamond near the river—little Mr. Krynos lying about being at the Nairobi airport. And Krynos had received something there from Gus Fisher—who was Smith's one-time pilot. Her head spun. Like a jigsaw puzzle that had been cut out of a cubist painting, no part fitted into another. And yet there *must* be some meaningful pattern. If only she could find it!

"Will you let me keep this pretty stone for a little while, Kandi?" she asked. The boy grinned happily and nodded Yes. "Now you run off and play."

Cherry found Jeff Jordan working on the water-filtering plant that he and Chuck had installed.

"Do you remember the stone Kandi found in the river that day?" Cherry asked. "The one I thought might be a rough diamond."

"Sure," Jeff said. He stopped tinkering. "But I told you this isn't diamond country. Why?"

"Well, what do you think of this one?" Cherry showed him the yellow stone.

Jeff looked at it for a moment. Then he held it up to the sun's light and squinted, with one eye shut. His face grew serious. He turned the stone round and round in his fingers, looking more quizzical all the time. Then he peered at her, his forehead wrinkled.

"Where did you get *this* one, Cherry?"

Cherry decided that for the time being she had better keep her confused thoughts to herself.

"Ask me no questions," she told him, "and I'll tell you no lies—don't ask me just yet, anyway. But what do you make of it, Jeff?"

"Well," Jeff said slowly, "I said that I was no trained mineralogist. But this looks to me like the real McCoy. If I had to make a wild guess, I'd say this is an honest-to-gosh rough diamond."

Cherry felt her heart pounding.

"What's all the mystery, Cherry?" Jeff persisted. "Where *did* you find this rock?"

"I'll tell you later, Jeff," she promised. "But just for

now, don't mention this to anyone for a while, as a favor to me. Will you? I have to do a little thinking."

She left Jeff shaking his head in puzzlement at the queer ways of women.

For the rest of the day Cherry debated whether she ought to talk this crazy business over with Bob. Then she remembered their ride out from Nairobi on the first day they came to Ngogo. She had told Bob then of the suspicions that were plaguing her, and he had pooh-poohed them. Of course, now she had what appeared to be a real diamond to add to the bits and pieces of the puzzle that lay in the back of her mind waiting to be put together. But maybe she'd better wait a little longer, she decided, to see what might happen next.

Cherry didn't have long to wait.

As she and Bob and Jeff listened to the safari news that evening, she sat bolt upright when the announcer said:

"Message for Dr. Robert Barton at Ngogo from the Abercrombie Foundation Laboratory in Washington, D. C. Query. What happened to the shipment of blood samples that you were supposed to have sent us by special MATS handling on the fifth? They have not arrived. Please advise."

"Now how about that?" Bob said, very much disturbed. He grew angry. "What happened? What went wrong?"

Jeff tried to soothe him. "Look, when you have an air transport service that goes all around the world you're bound to run into a few foul-ups."

"But blood samples, of all vital things! People are sick here!" Bob looked miserably at Cherry. "Whatever happened with that blood, it's bound to hold up the analysis a few days."

Bob flipped the radio switch to "send."

"Please get this message off to the Abercrombie Foundation, in Washington, D. C., from Dr. Robert Barton in Ngogo. Will investigate error in shipment at once. Please check at your end. Thanks, Operator."

Cherry tossed and turned in her cot that night, trying to form a clear picture from the formless thoughts running through her mind. But nothing came—no picture developed. Finally, exhausted, she fell asleep just as dawn was breaking.

"You look sleepy," Bob Barton said as they all sat down to breakfast. "And I was going to ask you to drive into Nairobi. Will your nursing schedule today permit it?"

"I'd rather not take time off," Cherry said. "The ward patients! Kandi's grandfather still has sweats and a high fever. You said yourself, Bob, that the teacher's child may need emergency surgery. How necessary is it for me to go to Nairobi?"

"It's urgent," Bob said. Cherry knew the doctor

could not go today. "I want you to check with Major Welsh at MATS and see what he knows about our missing package of blood samples. I'll lend you my Land Rover. You want Jeff to chauffeur you?"

"He needn't bother," Cherry answered. In a way she was glad of an unexpected day off. "It might be fun if I just drove in by myself. Don't worry. I know how to shift gears on a Land Rover."

"Yes, but watch out for the lions and rhinos," Jeff teased. "What would you do if one charged you?"

"I'd probably be just as scared as Long Jack Robertson said he was. But I don't think that's likely."

Driving into Nairobi all by herself was exciting. Cherry saw herds of zebras and giraffes cavorting across the broad plains. Once she passed a pride of lions, sunning themselves like a group of pussycats. Every now and then she fingered the yellow stone in the pocket of her jacket.

Once in town, Cherry drove directly to Eastleigh Field. She found Major Welsh at the MATS office. He was a freckled, very young man—almost too young to be a major, Cherry thought, except that the entire United States Air Force was young.

"Why, sure," the major said when she had explained her mission. "I remember that shipment. It came in here on the morning of—let's see . . ." He quickly leafed through a few papers attached to a clipboard ". . . on the morning of Tuesday the fifth. It was turned over to Captain Hagan, skipper of MATS 109, and he . . ."

The major looked up from the clipboard. "Say, here's a break. Hagan is here at the field right now in the 109, getting set for a take-off to the States in the morning. Let's take a run down to the flight line in my jeep, and we'll get the details from him."

Minutes later, the major's jeep, with Cherry sitting in the seat beside him, pulled up alongside a big jet cargo plane that was loading at one of the hangars.

"Will you please ask Captain Hagan to step out here," Major Welsh said to one of the airmen.

"Yes, sir!" The airman saluted briskly. A young redhead came out to the major's jeep.

"Howdy, Major," Captain Hagan said. "What's the word?" Then he saw Cherry. "Well now!" He took off his cap. "Nairobi is improving all the time."

"At ease," the major said, smiling. "This is Nurse Ames, from the Abercrombie medical project in Ngogo." The redheaded captain nodded and grew serious. "Look, Bill, we've got a problem. On last Tuesday you took a small package from the Abercrombie mission in Ngogo to be sent directly to the Abercrombie Foundation in Washington. Is that correct?"

"Right," Captain Hagan said. "I turned it over to Sergeant Morrison—he's our top crewman in charge of cargo—and he delivered it to its destination in Washington, D. C."

"Who gave it to you?" Cherry asked.

"Well," Bill Hagan said, "as I remember, he was a smallish type man with two cameras hung around his neck."

"That would be Ed Smith," Cherry said. "Dr. Barton entrusted the package to him."

"Well, he gave it to us all right," the MATS pilot said. "What is the problem?"

"The problem is," said Major Welsh, "that it didn't get to Washington."

"That's crazy," Captain Hagan protested. "We flew it nonstop from here to Dulles Airport in Washington. But let's see." He stopped a passing airman. "Ask Sergeant Morrison to come here."

Sergeant Morrison arrived on the double and the captain outlined the situation.

"Yes, sir," Morrison said. "The package was a small box, wrapped in brown paper, tied with a string, and addressed to the Abercrombie Foundation. I remember it perfectly."

"And you delivered it?" the major asked.

"Yes, sir. Just after we landed, a man came to the plane and identified himself as Abercrombie personnel. He said he had come to take the package at once—instead of having it go by messenger—and so I turned it over to him."

"You see, Miss Ames," Major Welsh explained, "under normal circumstances, a package like that—which isn't military equipment, and which isn't classified as top secret—would be delivered to its destination by our MATS messenger service. Since our planes don't operate on a tight hour-to-hour schedule as commercial airlines do, there would be no reason why the Abercrombie people would send a man out to get it. They would expect it on a certain day, but not at a specific hour."

"Excuse me, Major, Captain, but how did he identify himself?" Cherry asked the sergeant. "Did he show any credentials from the Abercrombie Foundation?"

"Well now, ma'am. . . . No, I don't reckon he did," the sergeant said. "He just said Abercrombie, and that he was expecting the package—that seemed like enough identification to me. He signed for it, and I turned it over to him."

"What was his name?" Major Welsh asked. "You said he signed for it."

"I don't remember right now, sir," the sergeant said, trying to think. "You see, we were unloading a whole cargo. And that one little package—well, I could get the man's name by going over the manifest for that day." The captain said he had better do that at once.

"Does the name really matter, Major?" Cherry said. "The right person didn't get the package. That's the important thing."

"You think some impostor did?"

Cherry murmured it was possible.

"But what would he want with a package of blood samples from your medical unit?" Major Welsh asked.

"That's what we've got to find out."

Captain Hagan asked the sergeant whether any other person claiming to be from the Abercrombie Foundation had come for the package. The sergeant said No.

The captain defended him—this was no error, but a clever trap. "I'm very sorry, but the sergeant and all of us did do our jobs," Captain Hagan said. "We'll trace the signature, and do anything we can to help. I hope that whatever has gone wrong will straighten itself out."

He saluted Major Welsh and went back to his job of supervising the loading of the 109.

"Now what?" Major Welsh asked.

"If you'll just take me back to my jeep," Cherry told him, "I'll go on into town." She felt very much disturbed.

"Any time we can be of help to you, Miss Ames, just let us know," the major said as he pulled up in front of the MATS building and handed her out of the car.

Back on the main street of Nairobi again, she drove to the headquarters of the Abercrombie Foundation. There she asked for Tom Gikingu. She was ushered into his office at once. As Bob had told her, Gikingu was a charming man, tall and lanky, immaculately dressed, with a humorous face and a clipped Oxford accent. He was, Cherry thought, the personification of the new sort of bright, youthful officials who had taken over the administration of most of the emerging African governments.

"Miss Ames!" he said, welcoming her with a smile. "How pleasant to meet you at last! Dr. Barton has told me all about the wonderful work you have been doing among my people. I have been planning to come down to see your hospital, and indeed had meant to do so this week. Please take a chair." He adjusted his heavy horn-rimmed glasses. "Now what can I do for you?"

Cherry decided that she had better not go into all the dark suspicions that were crowding her mind.

"Just two small things, Mr. Gikingu, if it won't inconvenience you too much." She took the yellow stone from the pocket of her jacket. "This stone was found yesterday by one of the children in our village. Our engineer says that it might—well, that it just *could* be a rough diamond." She handed it to him.

Tom Gikingu examined the stone as carefully as Jeff had done the day before, turning it over and over, allowing it to catch the light that poured in through the Venetian blinds of the windows.

"Well—well—well—" he said slowly. "You say this was found in Ngogo?"

"Yes, sir."

"I have never heard of any diamonds being found in that vicinity. Where was it discovered?"

Cherry determined to tell the truth—but not the whole truth—at least not right now.

"A small boy brought it to me. And since I was driving in to Nairobi this morning, I thought I had better turn it over to you so that you could have an expert examine it."

"Very interesting!" Tom Gikingu said. "I will have it appraised this afternoon. But you understand, Miss Ames, that if it *is* a genuine diamond, the State will have to impound it until a decision is made as to its disposition. I will be obliged to turn it over to the authorities."

"Certainly," Cherry agreed. "That is why I brought it to you. And when your expert has seen it, can you send me a message by radio?"

"Yes, indeed," Gikingu said.

"Oh," Cherry said, as though she had just thought of something, "there's one other thing. Are you familiar with *Click* magazine? It's published in New York."

"I read it every week."

"Then I wonder if you would do me a favor."

The African made a slight bow with his head. "I am at your service, Miss Ames."

Cherry was impressed, and flattered, by the man's courtly manner. "If it wouldn't be asking too much," she said, "could you cable the editor and inquire how long a photographer named Ed Smith has been connected with the magazine?"

Gikingu made a note on a memo pad.

"I will get the cable off right away. You will have your answers as soon as I can get them."

"I don't imagine that it would be a good idea to send those messages to us over the regular safari radio newscast," Cherry suggested. "At that hour, every safari party in Kenya and Tanganyika will be listening in."

Gikingu nodded. "You are perfectly right. It would never do to make any public statement about a possible diamond find—at least not until Government House has had an opportunity to make a thorough investigation." He thought a moment. "I shall certainly have answers to both your questions by tomorrow morning. Suppose we say that I will radio you direct at exactly twelve noon."

Cherry got up from her chair. "Thank you very much for your courtesy, Mr. Gikingu."

"Not at all. I am always at your service," Tom Gikingu said, bowing her out of the office.

On the drive back to Ngogo, a dozen weird notions raced through Cherry's mind. And slowly the pieces of the baffling puzzle began to put themselves together. But it was such a ridiculous solution that she couldn't believe it. She would wait until she heard from Tom Gikingu tomorrow, she decided, before mentioning her theory to Bob. She needed more positive clues.

She made herself stop thinking about the puzzle,

and concentrated on the changing colors of the landscape as the red African sun descended across the westerly sky.

Darkness was falling as she pulled the Land Rover up in front of the clinic. At the sound of the motor, Bob came out the door and down the steps.

"Well," he asked, "did the MATS people know anything about the missing shipment to Washington?"

"They're working on it," she replied. She reported the conversation to him. Tomorrow would be time enough to tell Bob her crazy theory.

The next day, a few minutes before noon, Cherry turned on the radio. Bob was busy in his lab and Jeff was nowhere in sight. At precisely twelve o'clock the speaker began to buzz and a voice said:

"KBC calling Nurse Ames at Ngogo. KBC calling Nurse Ames at Ngogo. Come in, please."

Cherry flipped the switch to "send."

"This is Nurse Ames at Ngogo. Go ahead please."

"Just a moment, Miss Ames, while I connect you with the Nairobi telephone."

Then an Oxford-accented voice came on. "Miss Ames, this is Mr. Gikingu speaking. I am replying to your questions of yesterday. One: The stone you brought me was genuine. The government mineralogists say it is a very valuable specimen. I have turned it over to them awaiting further information from you. Two: The following cable arrived this morning from the editors of *Click* magazine in New York. Quote: The photographer, Ed Smith, is unknown in this office. He is not now and never has been associated in any way with *Click*. Unquote."

"Thank you, Mr. Gikingu," Cherry said.

She put the microphone back on its cradle and turned off the set. Then, as an afterthought, she picked the mike up again and called KBC.

"Can you please put me on the telephone to Keeler's Camera Store? I'd like to speak to someone in the developing lab."

In a moment a man's voice answered.

"I am calling about some film that Mr. Ed Smith left with you," Cherry said. "He's a photographer with *Click* magazine in New York. When will it be ready for him to pick up?"

"One moment," the voice said. "Please hold the wire." In a minute or two the voice was back. "Did you say Mr. Ed Smith?" it asked.

"That's right."

"Sorry, miss," the voice said. "There must be some mistake. We haven't been doing any developing work for anyone of that name."

"Thank you," Cherry said, and cut the connection.

Outlandish as it seemed, it appeared that at last she had the answer to all the topsy-turvy events that had been going on ever since she and Bob had first arrived in Africa.

CHAPTER XI

The Test Tubes

ONLY MINUTES AFTER HER RADIO CONVERSATION with Nairobi, Cherry stepped into Bob's laboratory and closed the door behind her. He was alone, busily at work with a rack of test tubes that contained blood samples.

"Bob, I need to talk to you," she said. "Will you sit down for a minute?"

The young doctor frowned and cocked his head to one side, but he took a seat on the bench beside her. "Now what's all this about?"

"You've never thought that I was crazy, have you? Out of my head, or anything like that?"

Bob laughed. "Well, no, I hadn't. Maybe not until just now, anyway."

Cherry took a deep breath. Then she plunged in. "I think I know what happened to the missing blood samples that you sent to Washington."

Bob sat bolt upright. *"What?"*

"And I know that Ed Smith doesn't have anything to do with *Click* Magazine—and that he probably isn't even a photographer at all."

Bob was too flabbergasted to speak.

Then Cherry told him about her interview with Major Welsh and Captain Hagan at Eastleigh Field; about the diamond that Kandi had found in Smith's tent; about the message from Tom Gikingu on the radio; and about her radio conversation with the clerk at Keeler's.

"It all sounds too outrageous to make any sense," she hurried on. "But do you remember your friend Long Jack Robertson telling us that story about smuggling diamonds in the antelope head, the first day we met him in Nairobi? I think Ed Smith, and that funny little man, Krynos, and the pilot of the orange-colored airplane that sprayed the bush for us are all mixed up in some kind of diamond racket. The trouble was that I couldn't figure out how *we* came into it, but now I think I know about that too."

Bob sat listening incredulously, his mouth hanging slightly open.

"When you went to town to see Mr. Giginku and stayed overnight," Cherry continued, "the safari news had a story about an illegal diamond mining operation down across the border in Tanganyika. Then, about a week later, Jeff and I saw Mr. Krynos at the airport talking to the pilot, and we saw him take what looked like a briefcase from the plane. The next day Mr. Krynos showed up here, and shared the same tent with Ed Smith. And then, to top it all off, the package of blood samples that Smith took to the airfield was picked up in Washington by a man who said he was from the Foundation but obviously wasn't."

"And you think . . ." Bob searched for the right words, shaking his head in bewilderment.

"I think that somehow, some way, Smith managed to get some diamonds into that package of blood samples, which he knew wouldn't be subjected to close examination by the customs men at Dulles Airport. And a confederate in Washington picked them up."

"Whew! That *does* sound like you're crazy!"

"Just how it was all handled I don't know yet," Cherry said. "But if you'll do a little detective work with me, I think we can find out." For the first time during her long narrative, Cherry smiled. "Are you game?"

"You've just hit me with a ton of bricks," Bob confessed. "But sure—I'm game for anything, seeing that you've been playing Sherlock Holmes all this while by yourself."

"Speaking of Sherlock Holmes," she said, "he once remarked that when you have eliminated everything that is impossible, that which remains, however improbable, must be the truth. I think maybe that applies to us here."

"O.K." Bob grinned. "I've never read Sherlock

Holmes, but I'll take your word for it. What do you want me to do?"

"Now here is my idea," Cherry began. "Smith probably has some more diamonds hidden safely around here some place, ready to send to the States the first chance he gets. Otherwise, he wouldn't still be hanging around. Or maybe he figures on picking up some more from his contact, Krynos—or someone else. So when he comes back from his trip with the white hunter . . ."

As she went on outlining her plan, Bob kept nodding agreement.

Long Jack Robertson's truck pulled into Ngogo in the middle of the afternoon, and Ed Smith got out lugging his equipment. He greeted Bob and Cherry with a big smile and a loud "Hello, folks!"

"Hop down and have a cold drink, Jack," Bob said. "You must be hot and thirsty."

"Sorry," the hunter replied, "I'd like to, but I have to get my party into Nairobi by this evening. They decided to cut their safari one day short. But I'll be seeing you."

Jack waved his hand, turned the truck around, and drove out of the compound in his usual rush.

"How was the trip?" Bob asked the photographer. Cherry noticed that Bob was a good enough actor to keep any giveaway expression off his face.

"Magnificent! What scenery!" Smith replied. "I got

some pictures that I think are the best I've ever shot."

"Then I suppose you're anxious to get them into Nairobi to be developed as soon as possible."

"Oh, I'm not in all that hurry. They can wait until the next time you drive in."

"I was going to say," Bob went on, "that you could do me a favor. I have another package of blood samples that I would like to put on the MATS plane tomorrow. But unfortunately I can't leave here, and Jeff is tied up with work too. So I was going to suggest that you might borrow my truck and take them with you when you deliver your film to Keeler's."

Smith brightened at once. "Why, sure," he said. "I'll be glad to."

"Fine," Bob said. "I'll have them all ready by this evening, and you can leave first thing in the morning."

The sun was high in the eastern sky when Ed Smith climbed into the truck the next morning and started the motor. In the seat beside him, he had Bob's package, wrapped securely in heavy brown paper, and his own canvas bag.

"Anything else you need from town?" he asked cheerfully.

"Not that I can think of," Bob replied.

"Well, see you tonight." With that, Smith shifted the truck into gear and rolled off.

As soon as he was out of sight, Bob and Cherry got into the Land Rover. Both of them hated leaving patients to wait a day, but no case was so urgent that Kavarondi or Sara could not handle it for one day. And tracing the blood samples *was* urgent. Jeff, strolling around the corner of the hospital building, was surprised to see Bob and Cherry getting ready to leave.

"Are you folks going into town too?"

They had not taken Jeff into their confidence—on the theory that the more people who are in on a plot, the likelier one of them is to accidentally give it away.

"No," Bob replied. He carried his doctor's kit to make their trip appear medical, not a sleuthing one. "We have several errands all around here. We've packed some sandwiches and probably won't be back until late this afternoon."

"Well, if I'm not around," Jeff said, "it will be because I planned to take my rifle up to that little pool—you know, Cherry, where we had our picnic—and see if I can bag an antelope when he comes for his evening drink. We're starting to run a little short of steaks."

"O.K.," Bob said. "Good hunting!"

Driving down the trail to Nairobi, Bob took his time.

"If Smith is going to tamper with that package," he said to Cherry, "he'll stop somewhere along the road to do it. Not more than one or two cars a day travel along here, so he is sure to figure that he won't be disturbed. And we don't want to stay close enough behind for him to see our dust."

They rode along for an hour, neither Cherry nor Bob saying much, both keeping their eyes glued to the road up front. Then they rounded a bend—and there, about three hundred yards ahead of them, they saw the truck parked on the side of the trail next to a hedge of thornbushes. Bob had been driving slowly. He immediately cut off his engine and pulled silently over to the left of the road under the shade of a small grove of acacia trees.

Bob took a pair of binoculars from the glove compartment of the car and focused them on the photographer.

"I can't see very well because I don't want to take any chances of exposing ourselves," he said. "But he is sitting on the running board with our package in his hands." He handed the glasses to Cherry. "Here, take a look for yourself."

Cherry peered through the glasses. But her view, too, was obscured because she, like Bob, was trying to stay hidden—even at this distance.

They waited for more than thirty minutes, while Smith worked with the package. Then at last the photographer stood up, put the brown package back into the truck, got in, and drove away.

Once he was out of sight, Bob started the Land

Rover and they pulled up to the spot where Smith had parked the truck.

Cherry jumped out. "Look!" she said excitedly, and pointed to the bushes that lined the road.

The thorn branches were covered with blood that was still dripping from them in heavy drops; and little pools of blood had collected in the dirt, where it was still seeping into the hot and thirsty earth.

"He must have opened each test tube, emptied out most of the blood, and put the stones inside!" Bob said. "No wonder he didn't worry about the customs inspectors in Washington! It was a foolproof plan."

They climbed back into their car, and Bob stepped on the gas, kicking up a great cloud of dust behind him.

"Let's try to catch up with him before he gets to the airport!"

"Wouldn't it make a better case if we nabbed him just as he was turning over the package to Major Welsh at the MATS office?" Cherry suggested.

"Good thinking," Bob said. And he resumed a normal speed—about the same rate, he figured, that Smith would be traveling.

Then, just outside Nairobi, as they were passing through the National Game Park, a huge herd of antelopes raced across the road a few hundred yards ahead of them. They were impalas—hundreds of them—running in great, graceful leaps of twenty feet

"Look!" Cherry said excitedly, and pointed to the bushes

or more, blocking the road as effectively as though a freight train were passing by.

Bob jammed down on the brakes. For more than ten minutes they waited, until the last of the impalas had made the crossing and disappeared into the bush on the other side.

"Now we've *really* got to make time," Bob said, and he pressed down hard on the gas pedal.

It was a Saturday afternoon and traffic was heavy on Nairobi's main street. Bob fretted and fumed, constantly looking at his watch, as they inched along to the airfield.

"I wish I knew more about this town," he said impatiently, "so I could take a shortcut. But once I get off the main street and into the little twisty side streets, I'm lost. We'll just have to keep our fingers crossed and hope that the truck has been held up too."

At last they got through the main part of the city, and Bob raced the Land Rover along the road to Eastleigh Field. When they pulled up in front of the MATS building, Cherry saw the truck driving down a road at the far end of the airstrip. Smith stopped, leaned his head out the window, then quickly pulled it back in and gunned the truck around between two buildings.

"There he goes!" she shouted. "We missed him by minutes! And I'm sure he saw us."

The two of them scrambled out of the car and

rushed into the office. A secretary ushered them in to see Major Welsh, who was working at his desk. He rose to greet Cherry and Bob.

"Look, Major," Bob said breathlessly, "did my man Smith just deliver another package to you addressed to the Abercrombie people in Washington?"

"Why, yes, he did," the major said. "Only a little while ago. I've got it right here." He took the package from a desk drawer. "But in the light of what Miss Ames told us about the last one, I am going to have the flight sergeant demand positive identification before he turns it over to anybody when he gets to Dulles Airport."

"Have you a newspaper you're through with?" Bob asked as he quickly untied the package. "Or heavy wrapping paper?" Major Welsh found some for him.

Bob spread the paper out on the desk top, took one of the tubes from the cardboard box, and extracted the rubber stopper. Out came a dribble of bright-red blood, followed by a dozen or more bloodstained stones. A second tube yielded more stones. Major Welsh stood watching.

"Those look like uncut gems," he said. "Valuable?"

"Diamonds, Major," Bob said. "I'd like to get the local police on your phone!"

When he got through to the police station, Bob gave the sergeant a quick summary of the situation, and a description of the truck and its license number.

Then he kept nodding: "Yes! . . . Yes! . . . Yes!" and finally hung up.

"Smith won't get far. The police are putting out a dragnet for him," Bob told Cherry and the major. "He won't be able to leave the city limits. Maybe he won't even get far from the airfield." Bob wiped his forehead with the palm of his hand. "Man! What a day!"

Major Welsh picked up the cardboard box and the diamonds. "I'm going to take these myself to Government House."

"But what about Krynos," Cherry said, "and the pilot of the orange airplane?"

"I'm afraid we don't have a thing against Gus Fisher and Krynos that we can prove," Bob said. "Just the same, I'll ask the police to check them."

He called the station again and made this request.

"Tell them they can reach us at the New Stanley," Major Welsh said. "We need lunch, and we can talk there as well as here."

The major took the package of smuggled diamonds to deliver on their way to the hotel.

CHAPTER XII

Adding It Up

THE VIEW WAS SPECTACULAR FROM THE VERANDA OF the New Stanley Hotel. Over the tops of the city buildings, the high plains rolled away to the horizon, ending abruptly against the towering snow-capped peak of Mount Kenya. Cherry, Bob, and Major Welsh did not pay much attention today to the view. The MATS major was making notes; he would file a report at once. So would Bob.

"It was that evening in Cairo," Cherry was saying. "Krynos must have just happened to be in that café in Cairo; he couldn't have known we were coming there. And he happened to overhear us talking about our medical project in Kenya. So he came over to our table and asked questions—it must have occurred to him that we might be the perfect front for his diamond-smuggling operation. Do you recall how Mr. Krynos forced himself on us, Bob?"

"Yes, I remember your saying so after we left."

"And then there was that queer telegram that fell out of his wallet, mentioning the Mzabite and the order that was stopped. It gave me a creepy feeling that something odd was going on. Of course at the time I had no idea what it might be. Since then, I'd surmise that the telegram referred to the antelope head that the Mzabite taxidermist had stuffed with rough gems.

"So when Mr. Krynos left us at the café, he probably telephoned his accomplice Ed Smith in Nairobi, and asked him to look us up."

Major Welsh shook his head, then laughed. "The CIA or the Interpol boys ought to hire you, Miss Ames. You seem to have a natural nose for wrongdoing. But it's a pretty nose," he added hastily, "even if it is peeling a little from overexposure to the Kenya sun."

Bob said, smiling, "You are quite a girl to figure all this out. As far as I was concerned, I was a million miles away. Go on, Cherry. I want to hear it all."

"Well, if you remember—Ed Smith came along the first day we were here in Nairobi, and he introduced himself to us, right on this very porch where we're sitting. He didn't even know the name of the editor of the magazine he was supposed to be working for; and on top of that, he pretended to know a man that I made up on the spur of the moment. It was about then that Long Jack Robertson told us the disturbing story of the antelope head that was filled with smuggled diamonds."

"I hope you didn't suspect my old friend, Long Jack, too?" Bob said.

"Yes, I did, that evening when I saw Long Jack and Smith talking together here in the lobby. After I got acquainted with the hunter, and he seemed such a good sort, I wondered if that wasn't silly of me. But I did suspect Smith—rightly, as it turned out. Why, Smith was never connected with *Click* magazine— and since he never took any film into Keeler's to be developed, he probably isn't even a photographer. He was probably snapping an empty camera all the while, using that as an excuse to stay on in Ngogo.

"Then that first day at the clinic, when you, Bob, showed Smith the tubes of blood samples, and explained how you were going to send them to Washington by MATS planes, he saw his solution. He would put the diamonds inside the test tubes, telephone a confederate in the States, and have him pose as an Abercrombie man and pick them up. You remember that evening when he sent a radio message to someone—named Simon, as I recall—in Nairobi? The message went something like: 'I have my story idea figured out.' That must have meant he had found a foolproof way to get the stones out of the country. And my hunch is that Mr. Simon was actually Spiro Krynos, using another name."

"Miss Ames," Major Welsh said, "if I ever forsake

my career as an Air Force officer for a high-paying life of crime, I am going to stay several hundred miles away from you."

Cherry smiled but shook her head. "No, Major, at first I didn't really *know* that anything out of the way was happening. You told me, Bob, on our drive out to Ngogo that first day, that my suspicions just were due to the mysterious atmosphere of Africa working on me. So I tried to forget it.

"Then I saw Mr. Krynos talking to the pilot of the orange plane at the Nairobi airport—but both Krynos and Gus Fisher turned away when I called to them. And the next day Krynos showed up at our village, and denied that he had been in Nairobi the previous day. What was I to make of that?

"When Krynos showed up at Ngogo, you remember, he shared Smith's tent. How convenient for them! Krynos must have brought some rough diamonds with him—a lot of them—because little Kandi found one when he swept out under the cot. Possibly the gem fell off the table, unnoticed, when Krynos and Ed Smith were counting or examining the diamonds. Anyway, that's my theory."

"Do you use a pocket-size crystal ball, Cherry," Bob asked, "or a regular one?"

"Neither one," Cherry said, blushing slightly. "This is what my brother Charlie would call 'Monday morning quarterbacking.' Even that bloodstain on Ed Smith's sleeve after he had delivered your first package, Bob, didn't have any meaning until later, when we knew more."

A white-uniformed native policeman came up the steps to the veranda from the sidewalk, looked around, saw them, and walked over to their table. He saluted briskly, a swagger stick tucked under his left arm.

"Major Welsh? Dr. Barton?" They nodded. "Police headquarters asked me to report to you that Mr. Spiro Krynos took a BOAC jet out of Eastleigh this morning bound for Istanbul. He will be held and questioned by Turkish police when he arrives there. Your truck was found abandoned near the airport, but there has been no trace of Mr. Ed Smith. Mr. Gus Fisher, the bush pilot, has been interrogated, but he apparently knows nothing of any smuggling activities. He was released, but was asked to remain on call." The policeman waited. "Anything else, Major? Doctor?"

"Not at the moment, thanks," Major Welsh said. "I'll keep in touch with your office."

"Thank you very much," Bob said.

The policeman again saluted, did a crisp about-face, and left the veranda.

"Well," Bob said, "it looks as if we are just about where we were two hours ago. What's the rest of your story, Cherry?"

"I'm only guessing, you know," Cherry said. "Where was I? Smith—When little Kandi found that diamond under Ed Smith's cot, everything seemed to add up. I decided it just wasn't my overworked imagination after all."

"We still need proof," Major Welsh said. "But your account is entirely reasonable. It sounds complete, too."

"It does," Bob said. "It sounds as if you may have solved the big diamond mystery, Cherry, even though nobody yet has been nabbed for it. But I guess we can leave that to the police. Did I tell you that the police sergeant on the phone requested me to stay in town until tomorrow and explain all these details to the Kenya officials?"

"Then I'd better not leave the clinic unattended overnight, Bob." Cherry looked at her watch. "I'll be able to get back to Ngogo before dark."

Bob said he would feel easier, too, if at least one of them were on call there tonight. "It's a safe bet that Ed Smith won't show his face around the place. You take the Rover, Cherry. I'll pick up our truck from the police and drive out in that tomorrow."

"And I," Major Welsh said, "had better see that my planes keep moving out of here on schedule." He got to his feet. "Miss Ames, if we have any more mysterious goings-on in MATS, I'll look you up." He had a second thought. "As a matter of fact, I just might do that anyway. There's a dance at the Officers' Club next Saturday night. And maybe by that time you and Bob won't have so many weighty matters on your minds."

Cherry thanked him, saying it was not possible to answer now. Just then a safari car drove by, curving in and out of traffic as though the driver was in a hurry.

"Isn't that Jack Robertson?" Cherry asked.

"Yes, and he looks as if he's going somewhere in a rush. He must have a new bunch of clients coming in on the afternoon plane."

CHAPTER XIII

The White Hunter

THE SKY WAS BEGINNING TO DARKEN, AND THERE WAS a sharp smell of rain in the air, as Cherry drove the Land Rover down the trail from Nairobi to Ngogo. Now and then a thin spear of lightning cracked over the horizon, followed in a few minutes by a faint rumble of distant thunder.

Cherry recognized it as one of those sudden storms that come and go so quickly in the tropics. The few animals in sight were uneasy. A small herd of gazelles were huddled under a scattered grove of trees, and farther along the road a pride of lions lay close beside each other in the shelter of a huge acacia, their tails twitching nervously from side to side.

For the first time since coming to Kenya, Cherry felt apprehensive about the big beasts. What if one of them, spooked by a lightning flash, rushed the car? She wished that Bob, or Jeff, was sitting in the seat beside her. Or, best of all, Long Jack Robertson, with his big rifle across his knees. Then she shook off her fears as being foolish.

Soon a light rain began spattering the windshield. She closed the side windows up tightly and turned on the wiper. The raindrops made little spurts of dust as they hit the road. It would take a lot of rain, she decided, to turn the thick, dry dirt of the road into mud. But just the same, it might get slippery and tricky. She eased up on the accelerator and drove carefully, peering through the pie-cut shape of clear glass that the wiper made.

Then she saw a solid gray wall of rain advancing toward her across the level plain, obscuring everything behind it. It struck with the force of a massive blow that almost jerked the wheel out of her hands. The windshield became a watery blur. She braked the Land Rover to a stop.

The rain pounded down steadily for half an hour. Then, as suddenly as it had started, it tapered off to a light but steady drizzle. The red sun of late afternoon tried feebly to break through the murk. But even with the headlights on, Cherry could barely see the road ahead. She started the engine, and the wheels spun. They finally took hold in the gluey mire that the trail had become.

It was still five miles to Ngogo, and Cherry wanted to reach home before the sudden tropic darkness fell. She had hardly gotten the car rolling when a bright

orange plane flashed through the air, and she heard
the drone of its motor. The bush pilot's plane! Why
was he out in this kind of weather? She recalled that
the Nairobi police had given Gus Fisher a clean bill
of health, so far, in their investigation of Ed Smith.
But still—! Well, she thought, her problem now was
to reach the village without sliding off the road into a
ditch and getting helplessly stuck in the mud.

Driving was painfully slow. The day was growing
dark when she pulled into the compound at Ngogo.
The rising moon shone dimly through the rain-soaked
air—and by its faint light she saw the outlines of a
plane pulled up on the narrow beach. Even by
moonlight there was no mistaking the bright orange
color. It was Gus Fisher's!

What was Gus doing in Ngogo? The police in
Nairobi could have been wrong—or not revealing
everything they suspected.

All of her senses became alert. The back of her neck
prickled. Cherry got out of the car and moved cau-
tiously toward the steps of the hospital building.

The lights were on inside, and she could see the
tall, straight figure of Kavarondi moving around
among the patients' cots. Usually, at this hour, a few
people would be walking from hut to hut in the
compound, but this evening the sticky mud left by
rain was keeping everyone indoors.

She wondered where Jeff was. Then she remembered that he had said he was going hunting up by the

pool. Probably he had been caught there by the storm, waiting for a chance to bag a gazelle. She wished that he were here now. Everything was so spooky in the moonlit mist. And Gus Fisher's plane on the beach!

Cherry kept to the shadows as she moved around the hospital building toward her room in the back. Then she saw a dim light in the darkness. It was burning inside Ed Smith's tent!

She stepped behind the trunk of a large tree, to wait a minute until her heart stopped pounding, and to try to figure things out. From inside the tent she heard a murmur of voices, but she was too far away to hear what was being said.

Leaving the shelter of the tree's shadow, she moved toward the tent, taking each step carefully so that she would make no sound. Raindrops, still dripping from the trees, made a protective covering of quiet sound.

Reaching the side of the tent's opening, Cherry peeked inside. Ed Smith and Gus Fisher, the bush pilot, were standing beside the cot. Bending over it, adjusting the straps of a leather briefcase, was a tall figure wearing a faded khaki jacket and a wide-brimmed safari hat. The tall man straightened up and turned around. It was the white hunter—Long Jack Robertson!

Cherry gasped, and in her surprise she attempted to turn and run. But, turning, her foot slipped in the mud and she fell. The next thing she knew she was being helped to her feet and pulled inside the tent. Ed

Smith and the bush pilot stood glowering at her. Long Jack wore an expression of embarrassment—and shame.

"I'm terribly sorry, Miss Ames," he said, "that you had to find out about us. We thought the storm would hold you and the doc in Nairobi all night. I'm awfully sorry," he repeated, crestfallen. "But now I guess you know."

"O.K.," Ed Smith growled. "So now she knows. So what do we do with her?"

"Well," Gus Fisher said, "we can't leave her here, that's for sure. It was easy enough pulling the wool over the eyes of those two nurses at the hospital. But the minute we're gone, she'll be on the wireless to the cops in Nairobi."

"Then we'll smash the radio," Ed Smith said. "That ought to settle that."

"Now wait a minute," Long Jack Robertson said. "Use your heads. Sure, we'll smash the radio. But she could get to town in the Rover—or, if we fixed that too, she could send a couple of the natives here into Nairobi." He shook his head. "No, we'll have to take her with us."

"What?" Ed Smith's mouth was agape. "You're asking for a kidnapping rap."

Long Jack managed a feeble grin. "As far as I know, there is no such thing in Kenya. Besides, if we don't get clear of here with no traces, we'll all be up on diamond-smuggling charges, including your slick little friend Krynos. And there *is* a law—and a tough one—against that."

He turned to Cherry, who was trembling with fear.

"As I said, Miss Ames, I'm sorry you had to get mixed up in this sordid mess. But I promise you that nothing will happen to you if you just come with us quietly and don't try to kick up a fuss. We'll drop you off at some little village a hundred miles or so from here, and you'll be back safe and sound within a week."

"A week!" Cherry thought. "What will happen to me in that week?" But her words had died in her throat.

"That's a good idea," the bush pilot said. "We can land down in that little Warumbo village in Tanganyika—you remember, Jack—on the lake there. They'll take good care of her, and by the time she gets to a wireless set we will be in South Africa."

Long Jack picked up the briefcase, which he had dropped on the cot at Cherry's sudden appearance. Then he gently took Cherry by the elbow and steered her out of the tent.

"Just be quiet now," he said. "Then we won't have to be rough with you."

Cherry went along numbly as he led her toward the plane on the beach. The two others followed. All this had happened so suddenly that she was shaking. That Smith was a criminal she knew. That the bush pilot was in on it she had guessed. But the white hunter! She couldn't believe what her eyes and ears were telling her. She stumbled along as she walked, half held up by Long Jack Robertson's hand.

Passing the outdoor area where the two-way radio sat on a table under a protective covering, Ed Smith ripped off the cover and pulled out a handful of wires which he slung into the darkness behind him. "That takes care of that!" he grunted.

"We better put the Rover out of business too," Gus Fisher said. "I'll only be a minute."

When he returned, he informed the hunter, "I took off the distributor and threw it into the bush. So this place will be out of touch with the rest of the world for at least twenty-four hours. That will give us plenty of time."

"Good," the hunter said softly. "Now let's get moving." He again propelled Cherry in the direction of the river.

When they were only a few yards from the beached aircraft, Cherry was overtaken by wild panic. She made a desperate try to free herself, twisting away from the hunter's hand and wheeling around to run toward the safety of the dark trees. As she did so, she screamed for help.

Long Jack dropped the briefcase onto the sand and encircled her waist with a strong arm that felt like a band of steel. He clamped his other hand over her mouth, stifling her outcry.

The other two men stopped dead in their tracks. The pilot scooped up the leather case from the ground.

"Now, Miss Ames," the hunter said soothingly, "I told you not to make any noise. So come along now, and . . ."

"*Hold it!*" A voice rang out from the darkness behind them. Cherry almost sobbed when she recognized it as Jeff's. "Hold it right where you are and don't move! I've got a gun on you!"

Gus Fisher's hand snaked into the inside of his flight jacket and the shining barrel of a revolver gleamed in the pale moonlight. Before he could level the pistol, Jeff's rifle spoke with a red burst of flame and a loud crack that shattered the jungle silence. Fisher spun around, tripped over his feet, and fell into the sand. His revolver spun from his hand, arched over his head, and splashed into the water of the river.

"I said *hold it!*" Jeff's voice was hard. Both Long Jack and Smith had not moved from their tracks. Cherry disentangled herself from the hunter's arm. Turning around, she could make out the silhouette of Jeff's figure against the dim lights that shone from the hospital building.

"Cherry," Jeff said, "go have Kavarondi fetch a couple of the men. And while you're at it, get a roll of heavy adhesive tape from Bob's lab."

Jeff kept his rifle leveled at Ed Smith and Long

Jack, both of whom stood motionless on the beach, until Cherry returned at a run. Tomi and one of Jeff's big, muscular Kikuyu workmen followed close at her heels.

"Tape those fellows' hands behind them," Jeff ordered, tossing Tomi the roll of wide tape that Cherry had brought. When this was done, Jeff added, "Now go pick up the pilot and carry him to the lab. Unless I'm a worse shot than my father taught me to be, I only got him in the shoulder."

Ten minutes later Ed Smith and the hunter were sitting on the floor of the lab, their hands taped securely behind them. Smith had the snarling expression of a trapped animal. Long Jack looked miserable; he turned his head away from Cherry. The pilot lay stretched out on a cot, his shirt cut away from him, as Cherry examined his wounded shoulder.

"The bullet went straight through," she said to Jeff, "but apparently it smashed the clavicle—that's the collar bone. There isn't much I can do, except cleanse the wound thoroughly, until Bob gets here."

Fisher groaned as Cherry daubed at his shoulder with an antiseptic.

"With the radio and the Land Rover out of commission," Jeff said glumly, "that may not be until late tomorrow, or maybe the next day. He'll just have to lie there and take it. Serves him right." He had a sudden thought. "Wait a minute!" He turned to Long Jack. "Is there a two-way radio in that plane?"

"I was just going to mention it," the hunter replied. "As long as you've got us trussed up like Christmas turkeys, there's no point in letting Fisher suffer."

Jeff handed his rifle to Tomi. "Here, keep this on them while I go out and call the Nairobi police."

In a few minutes he was back. "Well, they've got a car on the way. It will be here in a couple of hours and Dr. Bob will be with them." He took the rifle from Tomi. "So you crooks just make yourselves as comfortable as you can. They are fixing up nice jail cells for you in Nairobi."

Cherry had given the wounded pilot a sedative and, with his shoulder bandaged, he was sleeping fitfully. The reaction from her frightening experience was catching up with Cherry, and now that she had done all she could for the pilot, her hands were shaking. She went to the refrigerator in the corner of the room and poured herself a glass of ice water.

"If you don't mind, Miss Ames," Long Jack Robertson said, "I could use a drop of that too."

After she had her drink, Cherry took a glass of water to the hunter, and held the glass to his lips. He drank thirstily. Then he seemed to relax a little bit, as though accepting his fate.

"I thought I was a pretty good hunter, young fellow," he said to Jeff. "But you outhunted me. Where did you come from out of the dark, and with that rifle? I looked the place over carefully after we landed, and there was nobody here but the Kikuyus."

"Oh, shut up!" Ed Smith growled. "You talk too much!"

Jeff had to laugh, but his laugh was a little nervous and high-pitched. "I was out hunting, trying to get us some antelope steaks. If the rain hadn't held me up, I wouldn't have got back in time to see you three dragging Cherry to your plane. I started to yell, then something told me to keep my mouth shut and come up on you quietly."

"Well," the hunter said, loosening up a little, "that's the instinct of a natural-born hunter. If I ever get out of this bloody mess, I'll take you out on safari." Then he added, "Would you believe me if I said there are no hard feelings? I should have known better."

"I said shut up!" Ed Smith growled again.

"There's no use shutting up," the hunter said softly. "I brought this on myself. And I learned long ago that people have to take their medicine when they make mistakes. So I'll take mine and be glad when the dose is down."

Cherry grew curious. Long Jack, like many men who are caught in a crime, seemed anxious to get at least part of it off his chest.

"I knew these other two here had a hand in the diamond-smuggling business," Cherry said to Robertson. "But how did you get mixed up in this? And why did you come back here after you knew an alarm was out for Smith?"

Ed Smith flushed with anger. "Shut up!" he snapped for the third time.

"No," the hunter said slowly. "I have every intention of making a clean breast to the police, so I don't mind doing the same with you, Miss Ames." He hesitated. "To answer your first question, I guess it was just plain greed. I thought I was a strong man, but apparently I wasn't strong enough to resist the lure of easy money when Smith here came to me with his proposition. He told me about the illegal diamond workings in Rhodesia, and in a moment of weakness—I suppose with a vision of a quick fortune—I agreed to be the go-between. As a white hunter, I had contacts all over East Africa and I could come and go as I pleased without arousing any suspicion. So I enlisted Gus Fisher and his plane, and we delivered the diamonds to Smith and his partner Krynos. They, in turn, were to see to the business of spiriting the stones out of the country."

Cherry's eyebrows went up. "Then you were in on that scheme to smuggle some of them to England in the horns of the antelopes you shot?"

The hunter smiled weakly. "Yes, and so was the man who posed as my client. He was one of Krynos' men too. But somehow, when things went wrong in London, he managed to give the police the slip. How he did it, I haven't any idea. Of course, as far as anyone knew," he added, "I was completely in the clear."

All the while the hunter talked, Ed Smith was silent, but glowering with hate.

Cherry persisted, now that Long Jack seemed so ready to talk. "But why did you risk coming back here tonight?"

"Well, for one thing, we knew you and young Bob were in Nairobi, and when it stormed so hard, we thought that you would certainly be held up all night. It would have been easy to explain our presence to the other people here—even to this young fellow with the gun—if neither you nor Bob were around.

"Besides that," he continued, "we knew the heat was on. Smith saw you two pull up at MATS headquarters just a minute or so after he had left the diamonds, so he knew the jig was up. He abandoned your truck and ran to Gus Fisher's hangar, and Fisher hid him in a tool closet while he got in touch with me. I drove to the field as fast as I could, and we had a quick conference. There was still a small fortune in diamonds in Ed's luggage here at the compound. I had given him a large consignment when he was with me those two days, and he'd only taken about a third of the stones to the airport to ship out with the samples of blood." He looked up at Cherry. "I wonder if I could have another glass of that water."

After Cherry had given it to him, he related the rest of the story.

"It was crazy, of course. We should have lit out fast

in the plane. That is what we decided to do as soon as it got dark. But when the storm came up, as I say, we figured you and young Bob would be trapped in town for the night, so we decided to risk coming back for the diamonds."

He shook his head as though to clear it of a nightmare. "Ed Smith insisted that we fly here first. I guess Fisher and I were panicky enough—or foolish enough—to agree. Neither of us is used to a life of crime," he said, again forcing a faint grin.

Then Long Jack closed his eyes, exhausted.

Jeff shook his head incredulously. He looked at his watch.

"Bob ought to be here with the police before long, Cherry," he said. "Why don't you get yourself a cup of hot coffee? Tomi and I will see that these crooks don't fly the coop."

"I think I will," Cherry said, grateful to get out of the room. She stepped out into the wet night and walked slowly around the hospital building for a breath of air. She would clean herself up in a little while.

An hour later, as she was doing routine chores in the ward with Sara—partly to work, partly to calm down—Cherry heard two cars roar into the compound. Bob came in, wet and muddy. He said he had had a furious ride in one of the police cars from Nairobi.

"Everything's under control," he said, smiling. He beckoned her to the door, out of earshot of Sara. "The police are taking charge of your prisoners. You can stop worrying." He put an arm around her shoulder, and patted her gently. "You've had quite a night of it," Bob said. "You shouldn't be working. Why don't you get some sleep? We can talk in the morning."

CHAPTER XIV

The End of the Story

A WEEK LATER CHERRY, BOB, AND JEFF SAT ON THE veranda of the New Stanley Hotel, within view of Mount Kenya. Its snowcap glistened in the hot morning sun. Bob had just returned from police headquarters, and the three of them were cooling off with iced cokes.

"Well," Bob said with a sigh, "I sure am glad that's over and done with at last. Now maybe we can get back to the normal business of running our hospital."

"I hope so," said Cherry. "I don't care if I never see or hear of another diamond again."

"Huh!" Jeff snorted, teasing her. "Maybe you feel that way now, but wait until you see a pretty one you'd like to wear."

Cherry smiled, but she did not joke back. She noticed Bob looked sober and reflective. He said:

"I certainly did hate to see Long Jack tangled up in such a filthy business."

"He seemed honestly sorry," Cherry said. "He made no excuses for what he'd done—except to admit that he had been tempted by easy money."

"There's no such thing as easy money," Jeff said. "Only some people, like our friend the hunter, have to find it out the tough way."

"I hope it doesn't go too hard with him," Cherry said. "After all, he told the whole story to Jeff and me, and he said he was going to do the same with the police."

"He did," Bob said. "And after he talked, Ed Smith broke down and sang a little song himself. When the officials mentioned the fact that sentences might be lighter if all the diamonds were recovered, Ed told the name of his contact in the United States—the man who posed as the phony Abercrombie agent and took the first shipment from the MATS plane. So the FBI got on his trail, and it looks as if they'll get back those stones, and very likely nab everybody else who was in on the deal."

"How about Krynos?" Cherry asked. "Did they ever find him?"

"Not yet. But Interpol—the International Police Force—are looking for him, and it will be a miracle if he can run away from them for very long. Obviously he was a phony, too, and not a trader at all!"

Jeff spoke up. "I didn't get taken into Miss Cherry-

Sherlock-Holmes Ames's confidence," he said, winking at Bob, "so I came in on this late. And, I might add, in a very surprising way."

"You were wonderful, Jeff," Cherry said. "The way you stopped those men on the beach was simply marvelous. If all this had been a movie, I suppose I would have wound up falling in love with you."

Jeff grinned sheepishly. "Well, it's not too late. Why don't you?"

"I may do it yet." Cherry smiled. "So you watch out."

Bob laughed. "O.K. When you kids decide to tie the knot, I'll be the best man."

Jeff realized that he was being kidded, and grew serious again. "What I don't understand is how Ed Smith knew beforehand that you were going to send blood samples back to Washington."

"He didn't," Bob said. "He explained that part of it when he spilled out the whole story to the police. But he was looking hard for ways to smuggle the stones out of Africa. Remember, the attempt to do it in the horns of the antelope Long Jack shot had gone wrong. So when Smith heard from Krynos that we were here on a medical mission, he decided to visit us—to see if he couldn't make use of some angle of our activities."

"And when he discovered, on his very first day at Ngogo," Cherry said, "that Bob shipped blood samples in test tubes to the Foundation in Washington, well—"

"It was a pretty slick trick," Jeff said.

"And if it hadn't been for Cherry's eagle eye," Bob said, "he'd have gotten away with it too."

"Oh, come on now!" Cherry protested. "My mother always warned me to beware of men who keep flattering a girl."

"All right," Bob said. "I agree with your mother. So I'll never say another flattering word to you again. How about you, Jeff?"

This time, when Jeff smiled, there was a faint touch of a blush under his tan.

"I don't know about that," he said. "It's pretty hard not to flatter a girl like Cherry."